LOST RIVER

A Western Story

Jane Candia Coleman

CHIVERS

British Library Cataloguing in Publication Data available

This Large Print edition published by AudioGO Ltd, Bath,
2012.
Published by arrangement with Golden West Literary
Agency

U.K. Hardcover   ISBN   97914713 1112 3
U.K. Softcover   ISBN   97814713 1113 0

Printed and bound in Great Britain by
MPG Books Group Limited

For Cisco

PROLOGUE

I heard the wagon and outriders approaching long before they came into view. Beside me, the boy spoke in a whisper.

"It's the dead wagon, missus."

I looked down at him, saw his eyes still red from weeping. "What?" I asked, startled and whispering, too.

"They come for the bodies. They always do, just like buzzards. But they won't find Pa. We fooled 'em this time."

Oh, yes, we'd fooled them, he and I, but as I turned my own wagon up the steep and narrow entrance to Lost River Cañon, I wondered where and how those men would strike next, and if, in coming here, I hadn't got more than I'd bargained for.

Only the day before, I'd witnessed the hanging of an innocent man, a gruesome sight I hoped I'd never see again. And tucked safely on the wagon seat beside me was my camera with photographs of the bodies the dead wagon had come to collect. What had begun as an adventure and a chance to enhance my reputation as a photographer had turned deadly.

I was beginning to learn that every thing — every place, every person — wears two faces, and that love and hate are joined together, capable of destroying each other. So it was in the valley of the Lost River.

My name is Sidra Givens, and this is my story.

CHAPTER ONE

My husband Edward died the year before I went to Lost River. He chose a good place to die, in a cañon where the old ones had lived in houses carved out of stone, and where their spirits still haunted the high walls, the turnings of the small creek that had once sustained them.

For two years Edward and I had been part of an archaeological team, photographing the ruins, recording each new discovery. It was, for both of us, provocative and exciting work, the more so for me because Lawrence Haslett, head of the expedition, had actually purchased several of my photographs to take back East.

Together he and I dug Edward's grave, and, when we had finished, he looked at me, his face kind and filled with concern.

"What will you do now? Will you be all right?"

Edward's death hadn't been unexpected.

We had come West hoping for a cure for his lungs even as he grew weaker, and, almost with his last breath, he'd urged me to sell out and go back home.

Except I had no home but the West where we had lived, loved, worked, and where I had learned the magic of seeing and capturing time by the simple act of looking through a lens and pressing a lever.

Edward had been a photographer, and he had taught me all that he knew. Standing there beside his grave, I remembered the first time I had watched an image come to perfection in the swirl of the developing fluid. I felt like an alchemist who had discovered the formula for gold. That I, too, could do such a thing, that I could make what was fleeting permanent gave rise to what I can only call passion. Oh, not the physical kind that exists between a man and a woman, though I am no stranger to that, either. What has driven me has been a consuming desire to possess the world — its stark beauty, the perfection of its existence, both cruel and sweet. What I have striven for is, I think now, an expression of self, my sometimes unbearable love of mountains, sky, and open spaces — glimpses of what, in the face of mankind, is honest and real.

What was real at that moment, however, was my sense of loss, the depth of pain that threatened to choke me. Edward was gone, and I was a woman alone in a vast and empty place.

Suddenly a thundercloud rose above the cañon walls, growing larger, feeding upon itself, dwarfing us as we stood beside the mound of earth, and it seemed that I stepped out of myself and saw us there — two small figures clearly defined against the brilliance — a man and a woman caught on the edge of change, the woman grieving but purposeful, filled with a hunger that had no name.

"I'll manage," I told Lawrence, knowing it was true. "Please don't worry."

"But I will. We can't just go off and leave you here." The team's wagons were packed and ready, had been for several days, but Lawrence had delayed the departure for my sake and for Edward's. I had always found him a kind man, but I was to learn that he had another, much harder side and depths that no one would ever plumb.

I rested on the handle of the shovel. "I'm going back to town. Our shop's still there, and I know how to run it. I'll be fine."

"Promise you'll keep in touch. Let me know if you need anything." Lawrence, as always, was tenacious.

"Yes," I said. "I promise." I wished he'd go, wished he'd leave me alone with the grave, the cloud, the voices of the old ones, my sorrow.

"I'll let you know what luck I have showing your photographs." He put his hands on my shoulders. "They're splendid, Sidra. You have a rare gift for seeing that has to be shared."

I nodded my appreciation and stepped away. There were times when I thought he acted too familiar, as if he owned me, or that part of me that was at the root of my passion, that place that even Edward had never possessed.

"It's going to storm before night," I said. "You'd better be on your way before the road washes out."

"Only if you come, too."

"Not yet." I stared down at the grave, the rocks, sand, shriveled roots of desert plants that covered it. "I'd like some time to say good bye."

"Don't stay too long. Life goes on, Sidra, though God knows it's hard sometimes." He bent and kissed my cheek, then turned and walked toward his team and wagon that was packed with treasures — clay pots, beads, primitive tools, fragments of yucca fiber clothing from a thousand years before — all destined for a museum far from their place of belonging. I watched him and the others out of sight and then sat beside the grave and wept.

CHAPTER TWO

The first fall and winter of my widowhood seemed endless. Although Edward and I had established a thriving business in town, it seemed that most people distrusted a woman who worked, regardless of the fact that I had no alternative. The only customers I'd had were roving cowboys who wanted a photo to send to their parents or give to a girl, and mothers with undisciplined children like the three-year-old who was squirming in the chair and scowling at me. Another minute and he'd be in tears, and both I and his mother were helpless to stop him.

"He's got to sit still." I came out from under the heavy, black cloth and spoke to the helpless mother. "Just for a little while."

"Sit still, Everett," the woman repeated. "You want a nice picture, don't you?"

Everett scowled harder, and I gritted my teeth and wished I were back at the dig, out in the desert, anywhere but in the shop where the cold wind was whistling through the cracks in the walls, and Everett was refusing to obey.

Edward had never had problems with children, had kept a toy box for the purpose of amusing them. I whirled around and ran to the closet, found a stuffed bear and lifted it over my head. "Here's a friend who wants his picture taken with you," I said to the little boy. "His name is . . . is Plush."

Everett reached out his arms, and I stepped away. "Plush will be very good as long as you sit very still just for a minute. If you don't, he'll growl. Loud!"

Everett giggled and clutched the bear and, a miracle, was still. I ducked under the dark cloth and peered through the lens. Boy and bear made a perfect shot. When the picture had been taken, I let out a growl. The boy was delighted.

"More!" he shouted. "More!"

"He may keep the bear," I said to his mother with a smile.

"You're so good with children. It's a pity. . . ." She stopped, realizing her error, but not before I was reminded of the fact that I had always wanted a child and now had neither child nor husband, only myself and a growing stack of bills which would have to be paid before I could go out and

14

photograph those things that fed my passion.

"I'll have the photo ready tomorrow morning," was all I said before I saw them out and locked the door.

The two rooms behind the shop where Edward and I had lived so contentedly were cold, and I poked up the fire and stood warming my hands. Perhaps I should have taken my husband's advice, sold out and gone home. At least there I would have had the comfort of friends, the security of the familiar. Instead I had chosen the harder way, determined to capture the world I loved. The fact that several times I'd driven out alone to visit my friend Lizzie Roanhorse and to photograph her as she sat weaving a rug before her loom had made me appear even more alien to potential customers. But whether bad for business or not, Lizzie's knowledge of place, and her re-telling of the old myths of her people, had added a new dimension to my love of the desert.

I thought with a pang of the dig in the cañon, how the swallows swooped overhead and the houses of the old ones seemed to have been abandoned only yesterday. I wondered then as I do now what will remain of our world, what shards, paintings and, yes, photographs, will be left to give clues to those in the future. Who might discover Edward beneath the desert soil and wonder, as I always have, about the fragility of life.

Lawrence Haslett had been one of the few who'd never laughed at my ambition, had, always, been full of praise. Would he, by chance, want me back on his next project? "I'll write tonight and ask," I said out loud, and felt the better for my small decision.

But Lawrence's letter arrived the next morning. It was short and to the point. **Dear Sidra,** it began. **Your photographs have aroused much interest here. In fact, there has been talk of an exhibit of your work at some point in the future. Meantime, I hope you will be able to join us again next summer at a newly discovered and, I believe, important site in the Lost River Valley. Your work has been invaluable. If you can come, let me know as soon as possible, and I'll send details and a check to cover your travel expenses. Your devoted friend and admirer, Lawrence Haslett.**

CHAPTER THREE

The camp wagon Edward and I had designed and built for work in the field usually brought stares and comments when we drove into towns, but in Lost River all attention was focused on the gallows that dominated the small plaza.

I pulled up just in time to see the victim die, to witness the faces of the crowd, some horrified, others gleeful, as if they'd been watching a circus act.

For once I was too stunned to think of picture taking and simply sat, the reins loose in my lap, my stomach churning. The custom of photographing the dead has, to me, always seemed particularly gruesome, and the hanged man, with his broken neck and ghastly, purple grimace, was no exception.

"Dear God," I mumbled to myself at last, and a woman standing close by looked up and smiled grimly. "Prayer won't help poor Harve now," she said. "Won't help the rest of us, neither. And there's Mercy with two kids, no husband, and no home to go back to."

She pointed at a tall woman with a lined and haggard face who stood near the gallows, her hands clasped as if in prayer. She must have sensed our attention, because she turned her head and looked at me. I had expected to see sorrow written in her eyes, even tears, but what I saw was anger, hard

17

and cold as iron and as indestructible. Anger and something else that bordered, I thought, on insanity.

"Lost her mind, poor soul, and whose to blame her?"

"That's enough, May." The man I judged to be my informant's husband took her arm, but she shook him off.

"No it ain't." She put a work-worn hand on the wagon seat. "If you come here to take up land, keep going," she said. "This valley's cursed, and you might end up like him, or scared half to death like the rest of us. I wish we'd never come, and that's a fact. All old Harve did was stand up to God-bolt, and see where it got him."

Not understanding, I shook my head. *God-bolt? I wondered. Who or what was that?*

"May!" The husband's voice was stern and, unless I was mistaken, frightened, but May was made of tougher stuff.

"I'm only sayin' what everybody knows." She gave a dry chuckle. "And here comes Nash Fallon lookin' like the no-good buzzard he is, but ain't that a face to stop your heart?"

I turned and saw a rider mounted on a tall black horse, riding so easily, in spite of the crowd, it seemed he and the animal were joined together in one fluid body. May was

18

right — he had the face of an angel, the features sculpted from some hard, pure stone, and when, for a moment, he looked at me, I saw that his eyes were blue — a very dark blue — the color the sea takes on at evening. I must have made a slight sound because May chuckled again.

"What'd I tell you? Handsomest critter a body ever seen, but no good, dearie. No damn' good a-tall."

"Who?" I asked. "Who is he?"

"Godbolt's hired gun. Come to clean us honest folks out so Godbolt can own the whole valley. Now don't say I didn't warn you."

With that, the husband yanked her away muttering something about "trouble", leaving me there in the plaza with the hanged man and a pair of ravens already attracted by the scent of death.

I watched them go, watched Nash Fallon move slowly away, and was reminded of Lucifer in all his bright radiance falling from paradise. It was then that I began to suspect that we, all of us, carry a hint of him within, and that we must struggle to preserve the good, defeat the evil, for without that, we, too, are doomed to fall.

I spent the night in the Oriental Hotel, a

splendid place, considering, and one filled with rumor and speculation. All the talk was of the dead man and of the cattle baron named Godbolt, who was, I gathered, determined to possess the entire valley as he already owned the town of Lost River, including the hotel.

There was a message from Lawrence waiting for me at the desk. It was brief and to the point. **My apologies for not coming to meet you. I've had some problems here at the site, but you will have no difficulty finding us. Just look for the Chastain Ranch and turn east up the Lost River Cañon. See you soon. Lawrence.**

Problems? I thought. It seemed the whole valley was fraught with problems, none of which was easily solved, and, although I hadn't expected to be met, the very lack of detail in the note bothered me.

What had Lawrence Haslett in his eager curiosity gotten us into?

A nearly full moon was rising over the mountains when I went to my room. It was a Western moon, clear and untarnished, and in its silver light I could see as clearly as if it were day — see the rock face of the mountains, the trees that lined the course of the Lost River, their tops turned to white fire

20

and moving as if in a dance. It was a peaceful scene, at odds with the events of the day, and it lulled me into a sense of security. In the midst of such beauty, there could be no violence of the kind I'd witnessed. And holding to that belief, I fell soundly asleep.

CHAPTER FOUR

From a high ridge I could see the entire southern end of the valley, trace the sinuous course of the Lost River that, in places, disappeared underground, surfacing a few miles farther on, swifter, wider than before. At times it reflected the sky, and at others it seemed dark, even sinister, shadowed by the cottonwoods and mesquites that crowded its banks.

Looking out, I thought I had seen few places more beautiful — the valley lush with grass, secure between mountains that were painted green, gold, purple where white clouds cast immense shadows. Not for the first time, I wished that film could capture color, for, while there is a stark perfection in black and white, it is the subtleties of color that amaze.

It was still early morning. The air was alive with the calling of doves, and the scent of the river was plain on the dry air. And then

I picked up the strong odor of smoke that lay on the back of my tongue, black and insidious, too strong to be grass or brush. Suddenly the peace was shattered by gunfire — several guns. I knew enough to recognize the sound of pistols, followed by several shotgun blasts, and after a pause two spiteful bangs from a .22 rifle.

Trouble seemed to be stalking me, or else I was being pulled into it — alone and helpless except for the pistol in my pocket that I'd never had to use.

In the heavy silence that followed, I remembered what Lizzie Roanhorse had said once. "White man hear guns and run to see. Maybe get killed. Indian hide. Listen. Watch. Sneak up later . . . or maybe run the other way."

Quickly I pulled off the road behind a clump of juniper. Beyond was a small depression where I halted the team and tied them safely out of sight. I got out my husband's .32-20 Winchester and, screened by brush, edged slowly to the edge of the incline.

I heard only the wind rustling the tops of trees. *Who had been shot?* I wondered. *And were they all dead?* My question was partially answered when the big black horse came toward me at a dead run. I recognized the rider as he thundered past me. Nash Fallon, obviously up to no good.

I waited a long time before I took the road again, driving slowly with the Winchester on the seat at my side. The smoke was stronger now, drifting through the brush, and above the waves of heat a buzzard was making a lazy reconnaissance. I clucked to the team and drove on — straight into trouble.

The house was still burning, its chimney sticking up through the flames like an exclamation point. Automatically I reached for my camera. It was one of the new Kodaks invented by George Eastman, easily managed because of its compact size and the fact that it used film instead of unwieldy glass plates.

Who had lived here? And where were they now?

For whatever reason, the scene I looked upon needed to be recorded — another decision that would bring trouble down on my head.

I climbed down from the wagon, leaving the rifle on the seat but shoving my Colt .41 into my pocket. A rough fence surrounded the small yard, and the gate was open, sagging on its hinges. Although the heat from the fire was intense, I walked toward it, focusing the camera on the burning house and attempting to ignore the stink of destruction.

I was so intent upon the picture that I stumbled and fell over a body lying in what had been an attempt at a flower bed. It was a man, bearded, his face rigid in final agony, his shirt soaked with blood. Three more bodies lay sprawled across the yard, one with a small hole in the center of his forehead.

Though I'd seen death, I'd never seen what guns could do to human flesh. I opened my mouth to scream, then shut it, frightened, when I heard the unmistakable sound of a rifle being cocked.

Someone I didn't know, possibly a killer, was hidden in the brush behind me. I felt for the pistol in my pocket. Edward had taught me to shoot, but I'd never been brought to the test, and, standing there, I wondered if I could do to another what had been done to the men at my feet. Slowly I turned around, clutching the camera in one hand.

The boy's face was black from soot and streaked with tears, but he held the .22 steady, and it was aimed directly at me. One glimpse of his eyes, blank not with fear but with hatred, and I froze in my tracks.

"Don't shoot," I whispered. "I won't hurt

you. It's all right."

The look on his face struck me to the heart. He was brave and determined, ready to fight me, or anyone, to the death. "All right!" His young voice sounded like a trumpet blast. "It ain't all right! It'll never be. Who're you?"

I spoke as quietly as I could manage, hoping to reassure him, but I realized that my voice was ragged and I was breathing hard. "I was passing by and came to help. What happened?"

He wiped his nose on a frayed sleeve, and left a smear across his cheek, but, when he answered, he was calmer. "I was out huntin' up our milk cow. Somebody let her out. My dogs was gone, too. I found 'em out there. Shot." He sobbed again. "I knowed something was wrong then, and cut for the house, but I didn't run right up like a derned fool. I sneaked up, and saw it all. The house was already burnin' when Godbolt's fellers come around front. Pa cut one down with his scatter-gun before they got him. I seen Ma run out and grab the gun and do for another one, but they cut her down, too. She ran back in the house. I don't know why. Maybe she didn't know what she was doin'." He gave an anguished glance at the now nearly consumed house,

25

then went on.

"There was two of 'em left. Nash Fallon and another guy. I drilled the other one right between the eyes when he turned around. I'm a good shot for my age, Pa said. I wish I'd got Fallon, but he run like a scared rabbit and I missed him . . . holed up behind the rock tool house. He stayed back there so I couldn't go help Ma out of the house without gettin' kilt and bein' no help to her anyhow. I watched till he run for it and I snapped off a shot at him, but missed. By then I couldn't get inside. I tried it twice, but it was too damn' hot."

His voice was coming out in enraged sobs. Who could blame him?

"The sons-a-bitches. I got one, and I'll get Fallon, too. Just wait and see if I don't."

I hardly noticed he was swearing, though such language coming out of a young boy normally would have startled me. I could cuss some myself on occasion.

Godbolt's wickedness is everywhere, I thought as I stood trying to comfort a child who had just had to kill a man.

"What's your name?"

He hesitated. "Jacky."

"Just Jacky?"

He looked uncomfortable. I waited.

"I ain't got a real last name. I was adopted

26

off an orphan train."

He started to cry, so I reached out and pulled him close against me. He went on, his voice breaking. "They wasn't my real pa and ma, but I always felt like they was . . . they was always real good to me right from the first. I don't know what my name was before, but I guess it's Chastain now."

My God, I thought. *So much trouble so young!* Then his name struck me. He'd said Chastain! The name from Lawrence's note. I was supposed to stop here for directions, but it seemed to me that the only direction from here was hell. Danger was all around us, a lurking presence — danger and the threat of violent death. I kept my arms around the boy and gave him a hug. To be twice orphaned and forced by circumstance into the rôle of killer was too big a burden for a child to bear.

He was skinny but strong, and, though he didn't return the hug, he stayed leaning against me, a small animal seeking shelter. I'd always longed for a son, perhaps not this one, but then God works in ways not always obvious.

"Did they have any kin? Your parents?" I asked.

"It was just them and me." He swallowed

hard, his Adam's apple moving above his collar.

The idea that came to me then was foolish, but somehow appealing. Although I was a widow with almost no money and in a strange place where people had been ruthlessly murdered, I was thinking seriously about adopting a child I didn't know. *Why not?* I asked myself. *We're both alone.*

Out loud I said: "My name's Sidra. Sidra Givens. And we should bury your pa."

He shook his head and kicked at the ground. "We could dig all day and not get done, missus. This here's caliche. We could be diggin' and have 'em come back and try again. And . . . and there's Ma still in there."

If there was anything left of his mother, we'd not recognize it. Perhaps in a day or so I might go into town and find a minister or priest to come say some words over the ashes, but my immediate problem was what to do with the boy, especially if, as he'd said, the killers would come back and try again. Certainly I couldn't run off and leave him there alone with his grief and four bodies. It would be like deserting a puppy, even though he'd proved himself to be both capable and tough.

"We should report this to the sheriff," I

28

said at last.

Jacky's jaw dropped. "I ain't goin' to that old buzzard, and, if you're smart, you won't go, neither. You don't know how it is here. The sheriff's a crook and in Godbolt's pocket just like everybody else. I'll hide out somewhere and take care of the place like Pa would've wanted."

I pictured him burrowed into a cave in the hills, foraging for food, stealing when all else failed, and my heart turned over. I knelt down so our faces were level. "Jacky," I began, unsure how to convince him of his youth and vulnerability, "will you come with me to my friends? They're the men at the dig in the cañon, and that's where I'm headed. We'll take your pa with us in the wagon, and I'm sure Doctor Haslett will know what we should do."

His eyes brightened, and for just a second I glimpsed the boy that he was behind his hatred and sorrow.

"It was Pa and me that found that place," he said. "It's on our land, and we run our cows up there in summer. Sometimes we'd just go up and hunt for stuff. We found arrowheads and a bowl we gave to Ma as a surprise. We guessed it was near a hundred years old, but Doctor Haslett says closer to a thousand."

"You know Doctor Haslett pretty well then?"

He nodded. "He met Pa haulin' wood to the train station last year, and got so excited over what Pa told him he come right out to see for himself. That's how come he's here." He stopped, obviously thinking and a lot more inclined to trust me. Finally he said: "Sure, I'll go up there with you. But maybe he won't want me. You'll have to hide me out 'cause Fallon knows I killed his man. They'll be after me."

I hadn't thought that far ahead and wondered what Lawrence would say when I dragged in a fugitive, even a small, orphaned one. There were times, as I knew very well, when Lawrence's Puritan streak blinded him to anything else.

Well, I thought, *you'll just have to accept the situation, Doctor Haslett. If you don't want him, you don't get me. I'll go on the dodge with him because he can't do it alone.*

Jacky said: "Maybe . . . if Mister Haslett will have me" — he frowned, thinking — "maybe there's a job I can do and still keep an eye on this place. I have to keep the place for Pa. You understand?"

I did. He was loyal and earnest even if he couldn't comprehend the trouble that had, as I saw it, only begun, but at least he'd agreed to come with me. At least he wouldn't be alone.

"I'm sure Doctor Haslett will have some suggestions," I said, getting to my feet and taking a last look around at what had once been a happy home. "If you'll go get me the canvas that's just inside the back of the wagon, we'll cover your pa and carry him in it."

Jacky went off, rifle tucked under one arm, caution bred into him and made all the more necessary by what had happened. Although I had always hated the practice of photographing the dead — infants with their sweet eyes forever closed, those who'd died from an illness or from old age, shrunken and pale in their coffins — the scene around me was different, and the bodies. What had happened here was murder, the evidence plainly visible.

Quickly I picked up the Kodak, shot the dead sprawled on the trampled ground, the house still smoldering, the black ash incongruous in the brightness of the morning.

"What're you doin'?" Jacky came toward me, dragging the canvas.

"Making a record in case it's ever needed," I told him. "This was arson and murder, and the pictures will show that."

His eyes grew round. "You'd better not

31

tell nobody you did it."

"Don't you, either."

"Pa taught me to keep my mouth shut. There's things happen nobody needs to know."

He looked like a little old man standing there, rifle still under one arm. *Too soon,* I thought. *He's grown up too soon,* and hated the fact that I wouldn't be able to get his pa's body into the wagon without his help.

But together we managed the gruesome task and dragged the bundle to the wagon, then used the planks that Jacky found to pull him inside. Joe Chastain had been a large man in life. Dead, he seemed larger, a heavy and unco-operative burden. Several times I had to stop and catch my breath, fearful that he'd roll off the planks and we'd have to start all over. When the body was stowed on the floor of the wagon, I leaned against a wheel fighting nausea. There was blood on my hands, on my skirt, and the smell of death mingling with the acrid smoke was almost more than I could bear.

Jacky, however, was thinking. Without a word he collected the weapons that lay scattered on the ground and, when he saw me watching, gave a shrug.

"No sense leavin' 'em here. We might need 'em."

"What about . . . them?" I gestured toward the slain men.

His face turned hard, not a boy's face at all for just a moment. "Their own kind'll come fer 'em. They don't deserve nothin' from us." As he said it, he looked like he'd like to kick their bodies.

I felt suddenly worn out.

"Then let's go," I said, and slowly climbed to the seat and unwrapped the reins.

He hopped up beside me.

"The road's right yonder."

We'd just turned into the cañon when we heard another wagon coming. I'd learned my lesson and quickly pulled into a small, brush-covered gully.

Jacky jumped down. "You stay here out of sight. I'll get a couple more, if they come up here." The look in his eyes, that of a man for just a moment, suggested I'd better do as he said.

He was back in a few minutes.

"Who are they?"

That's when he told me about the "dead wagon".

CHAPTER FIVE

He led me up the gully to an outcrop of rock on the crest of the hill. From there we looked down on the ruined yard and the dead wagon stopped inside the fence. Beside me, I could feel Jacky seething as two men got down and walked around, obviously searching for something.

"Probably lookin' for Pa's body." Jacky made a sound that should have been a laugh, but there was no humor in it. "If they come up here lookin', I want you to let me use that rifle of yours. If I had Pa's Forty-Sixty, I'd bag them from here."

After what he'd told me, what I'd seen for myself, I thought I'd probably help him, but I didn't answer, just watched as the two men piled the bodies into the wagon bed.

Although in the next weeks I was to become inured to killing, that day I was still innocent enough to think that those bodies had been alive only a short while before, and that once those men had been kids, like Jacky, with mothers who would always wonder why their sons never came home again.

"Why do they do such a terrible thing?" I whispered.

Jacky looked down at his hands, clenched into fists. "When Godbolt wants your place, his men come, and then the wagon comes for the bodies. They get rid of 'em somewhere, prob'ly on old Godbolt's ranch, but nobody knows for sure. Nobody they killed was ever found."

He sobbed once, then stifled it. "Guess they'll never find Ma, either."

Below us, the men continued their search, walking in a widening circle. Occasionally we caught a word or two when they raised their voices, but for the most part all we heard was wind and the rustle of grasses.

Jacky broke our silence at a thought the dead wagon's presence probably brought to his mind. "They found old Granny Prosser dead on her porch last year. Folks say Nash Fallon come around and shined up to her, then, when she kinda got to actually like him, poisoned her tea, but couldn't nobody prove it. All we know for sure is that now Godbolt's running cows on Granny's place. But he don't like to leave any evidence like happened in her case, or witnesses, neither."

"But he left you."

The enormity of what I'd said stunned us both. Jacky was alive to point the finger, and in my camera were the photographs to back him up. As long as we were alive, we were a threat to the man and his crimes.

With that, I discovered how quickly the innocent can become the victims and learn to conceal themselves. It wasn't fair, but then life hadn't been fair to either of us.

What were the two men saying to each other in that sad and ruined place? Were they, perhaps, admiring Jacky's splendid shot, right between their friend's eyes? Or had they decided to search further for Joe Chastain's body — and perhaps even discover my wagon tracks that led plainly out of the yard and up the cañon? And what would the man named Godbolt do when they reported the missing body to him?

I watched as at last they climbed up on the wagon seat and drove away with their ghastly load. *Buzzards,* I thought. *Nasty, evil, stinking things!* — and with that let out the breath I'd been holding. If they'd discovered us, I had no doubt that Jacky and I would have had to fight it out with killers. For there was no doubt in my mind that Jacky's life was in danger.

Despite the horrors I'd just witnessed, the astonishing beauty of the cañon touched me deeply, aroused emotions I could hardly explain or capture. Beyond the narrow entrance, the trail twisted, then widened gradually as if in welcome, the rock sides farther and farther apart but towering over us. At their height, the wind had played sculptor, carving spires and hoodoos that stood like silent guardians, their heads seeming to touch the sky.

The trail we followed was little more than a cattle path through grass as high as the wheels of the wagon, and on the lower slopes of the mountain, poppies, millions of them, blazed like fire.

For the first time since Edward's death I felt the old desire, that communion of nerves, senses, and place that has always driven and inspired me. I hungered for the moment, hungered uselessly, for no method existed to capture the golden bronze shimmering of flowers, the music of creek water over stone, the red and yellow lichens painted on rock.

Whoever had lived here must have been dazzled, dazed by color and contrast, stunned into silence by the blue sky balanced on the shoulders of the mountain, regardless of the hardship of their existence.

I imagined women grinding nuts and corn on stone *metates,* and children laughing as they splashed in the creek. I saw men returning from the hunt with their quarry, a deer, perhaps, or a sharp-tusked javelina, rabbits whose fur would be made into soft blankets, warm robes.

Food, shelter, water, and the watchful hoodoos standing look-out above. "Paradise," I said, knowing I would carry this vision with me.

Jacky, practical and of the earth, only grunted. What he saw was food for cattle, riches of another kind, but perhaps, I thought, I could widen his perceptions, pass on those things too intangible to be captured. Perhaps.

"Why'd we stop?" he asked.

"I was thinking about who used to live here all those years ago."

"Was it like now?" he wanted to know, curiosity lighting his eyes.

"Probably," I said. "I doubt the cañon has changed much."

"Then where are they? Why'd they leave?"

It was a good question, and I took my time answering. "We don't know. At least I don't. Doctor Haslett has theories, but that's all they are. The fact is, there were villages and people all over the West a thousand years ago, but they're gone, and it's a mystery what happened. Some say drought or disease killed them, but other people think they were driven away or murdered by their enemies."

"Like now," he said, the light fading from his face.

"Sort of. There have always been bad people trying to take what's not theirs. It's how people are."

38

"It stinks." He hunched his shoulders as if he was cold. "Why's it have to be like that? Why can't folks just mind their own business?"

I was sitting in a cañon trying to discuss morals and ethics with a small, bereaved boy — a child I hadn't even known until a few hours before. Strange, indeed, but in another way hopeful.

"Because," I said slowly, trying to simplify logic. "Because if everybody and everything was good, we wouldn't recognize it. It's like we need the bad for balance. To make us understand. To keep us honest, in spite of evil. It's the battle between God and Satan repeated over and over, you see."

And then I thought of Nash Fallon whose beauty had struck me dumb, and how he had killed without mercy. I sighed, and Jacky said: "You sound like a preacher, but I guess . . . I guess I know what you mean."

"It's a hard lesson." I tightened the reins and the two mares lifted their heads, their mouths filled with the long grasses. "It's hard, and I'm sorry you had to learn it so young."

He gave me a bleak look and hunched into himself again. "Missus," he said, "I reckon I learned it a long time ago. Before I ever come here."

For that, I had no reply.

Instead of the orderly camp that Lawrence always insisted upon, Jacky and I drove into chaos.

The crew was trying to right the tents that looked like they'd been blown over, their poles smashed, the canvas torn, while Lawrence was shoveling out what had been the beginnings of the dig. When he saw us, he jabbed the shovel into the dirt and walked to meet us, his face grim.

"What happened?" I asked as he helped me down.

"Somebody stampeded a herd of cattle through here like the devil was chasing them. Rode right across my stakes and the dig, and kept on going with not so much as a hello."

"Who?" I began, and then knew. "Don't tell me. All I've seen and heard for the past two days has been the doing of some person called Godbolt. First a hanging, then Jacky's folks, now this."

His hand tightened on my arm. "What about the Chastains?"

I told him, moving away from the wagon where Jacky sat holding the team. When I'd finished, Lawrence exploded.

"By Christ, Sidra! This is madness beyond belief! Things don't happen this way!"

I almost laughed. "It seems that out here they do."

He had the temper to match his red hair. "Running roughshod over the site is one thing, but murder's another, Sidra. You and I and Jacky are going to the sheriff right now."

"We aren't, either," I said. "Jacky says that this Godbolt person controls the sheriff. We have to hide him out and keep quiet until we know what we're up against. Believe me, if you'd seen the dead wagon, you'd know what I'm saying."

"The what wagon?" The expression on his face made me laugh again, though the situation was far from funny.

"And I got you into this," he said when I'd finished explaining. "Dead wagons, killings, house fires. But God, what a find this place is! There's a whole city buried here. It needs to be excavated, mapped, preserved, and that bunch that came through yesterday should be thrown in jail. But I still think we should go to the sheriff. He's the law, isn't he?"

"Don't be naïve!" I snapped. "My life's on the line, too, and I'm not sticking my neck out any farther. For right now we have

41

to get rid of Chastain's body before some-body turns up and finds him, and then we have to think about hiding Jacky. But none of this means going to the sheriff."

"Missus!" Jacky's voice was low and fright-ened.

We turned and saw a surrey coming up the cañon, saw the driver, a man thin to the point of emaciation and dressed in black, flicking a long whip, hurrying the lathered horse.

I knew who it was without asking, knew with a kind of dreadful intuition that the creature hunched on the seat was none other than Godbolt.

I edged over to the wagon where Jacky had hidden himself. "Stay in there and don't come out. We'll handle this." And I hoped desperately that he'd not take it into his head to shoot Godbolt, for he was angry enough to do it.

CHAPTER SIX

Even if I'd known nothing about the man, instinct, that warning system passed down from early ancestors, set up all my defenses.

Godbolt drove up, and he was smiling, but the smile did not, could not, touch his eyes. Depthless, gray, triangular in shape, those eyes reminded me of a rattlesnake's. I took a step back and bumped into Lawrence, then stood unmoving, as if awaiting a sentence — life or death.

He took off his hat, bowed to me, and, bending over, extended a hand to Lawrence. It seemed he wished to stay in a position where it was necessary for us to look up at him.

"Colonel Abner Godbolt," he said in a resonant voice at odds with his almost emaciated body. "I understand you had some trouble here."

"As you can see." Lawrence gestured at the tents and the churned-up earth, then introduced himself. "Doctor Lawrence Haslett from Washington. And this is Missus Sidra Givens, our photographer."

Godbolt swept me with a glance, then returned to the reason for his visit. "My men weren't to blame. They were moving a herd off bed ground when somebody, probably some of my enemies, stampeded it. But I'll pay for whatever damage was done."

Lawrence had stepped in front of me, trying, I supposed, to hide the evidence splattered on my skirt. "No need for that, Colonel, if that's the case. I just hope it doesn't happen again. This is an important site. Maybe as important as Chaco or Mesa

Verde, and I'll need the co-operation of everybody in the valley."

"You can count on mine," Godbolt said. "I can't speak for the nesters." He looked at me, the snake again. "And you're a photographer? I suppose you document each . . . what do you call them? Discovery?"

I chose my words carefully, fearful that I'd slip up somehow and give us all away. "The important ones. I make a continual record of each unit as it's excavated, and of the artifacts we find. I also take photographs for sale and exhibit."

I'd seen his eyes on my skirt, but he chose not to mention it. He'd also taken in the wagon with the sweated horses, and my camera perched on the seat. I suspected that his appearance was prompted because he'd been following the dead wagon, seen my tracks, and followed them right to camp. And if I knew anything, it was that Fallon had met him and was somewhere close by, ready for trouble.

But the colonel was clever, concealing any evidence of his knowledge. Abruptly he said: "Would you consider coming to the ranch and photographing my daughter? I'd pay, of course."

Was it a trick? If he had already made his decision, I could be walking into a death

44

trap. I hesitated, and he read my doubts.

"Come now, Missus Givens. No matter what you've heard, I don't bite. I'm giving a reception for Celine. She's eighteen, and I promised her mother many years ago that she'd come out. Perhaps you would both like to come?"

I looked at Lawrence, hoping to be saved from what I could only imagine was a trap, but to my surprise he accepted. "We'd be delighted. That way we can meet some of the neighbors. And Sidra's taken some fine portraits. You won't be disappointed."

"I never am," came the answer. "A week from today, then. Celine will look forward to it." He picked up the reins as if to leave, then turned back. "You haven't seen anything of the Chastain kid, have you?"

Though he spoke casually, his purpose in coming was now obvious. I bit my lip, and realized too late that all of Lawrence's protective instincts had been aroused, as well as his famous temper.

"After this morning, we may never see him. It's a damn', bloody shame what happened down there. Whoever killed those folks ought to get a taste of their own medicine. I was telling Sidra we should go to the sheriff. I still think so."

I couldn't believe what I was hearing, or

45

that Lawrence could be so stupid.

Godbolt's face turned to stone. "There's no need for that."

"Why not? Joe didn't burn down his own house and shoot himself. It's pretty plain what happened."

"You were there, Doctor Haslett?"

"No, but Sidra was."

Tell him something he doesn't already know! I thought. In his reckless anger, Lawrence had put to rest any doubts this dangerous man may have harbored — made me a target. I fought my own anger then — at Lawrence for being a fool, at the colonel who reeked of evil, and at myself for trusting anyone.

"Is that true, Missus Givens?" Godbolt sounded like the lawyer for the prosecution.

Lawrence might have betrayed me, but I'd be damned if I'd betray myself. "It was over when I got there. All I saw was the house in ruins and the dead men."

"How many?"

Oh, he was clever. I gave him that, but refused to answer, taking refuge in femininity. "I . . . I don't know. I was frightened. I just wanted to get away. I ran, and . . . and fell over a body and got my skirt bloody."

"I see."

"Yes," I said. "I'm sure you do."

46

"In other words, you think those were my men."

I didn't answer directly, still protecting myself as best I could. "I wouldn't recognize your men," I said. "I'm new here."

"I wouldn't let my men do such a thing," Godbolt said, proving he could tell a lie without blinking. "Whoever burned out the Chastains is probably part of the gang that stampeded my cows. Nesters. They're organizing against me. I think they've even pooled their money . . . what little they have . . . to bring in hired guns. I'll report this to Sheriff Briscoe. He'll be very interested in what you've told me."

That sounded to me like a subtle threat, and I said nothing.

"And if you see the kid, bring him to me." It was a command.

"Why?" I asked, just to be contrary, as though we all didn't know too well.

"So I can take care of him, Missus Givens. He's an orphan now."

I forced a smile. "That's kind of you," and thought — *We know how you want to "take care of him" all right.*

He replaced his hat. The wide brim shadowed his eyes, but I'd seen their malevolent glitter and knew he'd caught my sarcasm. "I get what I want," he said. "If you're here

47

long enough, you'll find that out."

When he'd disappeared down the trail, Lawrence let out a whistle. "You made an enemy, Sidra."

I wanted to slap him silly. "He was already an enemy! You tenderfoot, he followed my trail right here. He already knew. And if he had any doubts, you removed them."

"I wasn't thinking. He got to me the way he questioned you and asked about the boy."

"Well, dammit, you'd better start thinking! It's bad enough we've got Jacky to hide and his pa to bury. Not to mention a whole roll of pictures. Now I've got to watch my back trail because you couldn't think!"

He looked as if I'd punched him. "You've got what?"

"Photographs. House . . . bodies . . . all of it. It's evidence, even if they do get me. But let me tell you, they'll have to catch me first. And the only reason I agreed to go to his daughter's damn' coming out party was that I doubt he'll try to murder me in front of the whole valley."

"Who else knows about the pictures?"

"Just you. And Jacky. But I trust *him*. He's been around long enough to know to keep quiet. Not like some I could name."

He ignored that with difficulty. "Let's keep it that way. Get the photos developed, and we'll send them to my office back East. They'll be safe and so will you. I'm sorry, Sidra. I never meant to put you in jeopardy. But we'll all keep our eyes open. You and Jacky can count on that."

Abruptly I changed the subject. "I've half a mind to file for his guardianship," I said.

The frown lines between his eyes deepened. "You're a single woman. No court's going to approve that."

His tone irritated me. "Is being single a crime?"

"Of course not. But it's obvious Godbolt controls this county, and you can bet he'll be standing in the wings watching and waiting to snatch the kid. My advice is to just bide your time. We don't know what'll happen."

Although I hated to admit it, he was right. Once again, though, intuition told me it would be a long time before any of us were safe from harm.

CHAPTER SEVEN

"Blabbermouth!" Jacky jumped out of the wagon and ran at Lawrence. "You had to tell! I thought you were smart, but you ain't. And now you're goin' to that old bastard's party! You're throwin' in with him!"

49

"Jacky, you shouldn't talk . . . ," I began, but he cut me off.

"Pa told me not to trust anybody, and he was right. *Anybody* can't keep *his* mouth shut, ain't to be trusted."

"Now, hold on." Lawrence reached out and grabbed the boy's arm.

When he used that tone, it commanded respect, as I knew. He was in charge and expected instant response — from Jacky or anyone else — and usually got it. Reluctantly the boy quieted down, though he tried to snatch his arm away and refused to look at either of us. If Lawrence hadn't kept a hold on him, he'd probably have run away.

Lawrence squatted beside him and went on more gently. "I made a mistake. I admit it, and I feel bad about it."

Jacky's scowl began to evaporate as soon as he heard a grown man admit a mistake. Few had in his experience, I'd bet, or in mine, either.

Lawrence noted Jacky's expression, too — had been watching for it — and he continued: "I don't only feel bad for me, but because of you and Sidra. But mistakes happen. Your parents were my friends, and I hate what was done to them as much as you do. I lost my temper and said things I shouldn't, but I aim to keep you and Sidra

50

safe, and that's a promise. She and I might have to do some things you won't understand, play along with Godbolt to fool him, but I'm hoping you'll trust us. You can ask anything you want, but I don't expect accusations from you. Is that clear?"

Jacky looked to me for a signal.

"Sometimes people get carried away," I said. "And sometimes people have to act for a while against what seems right in order to do right in the long run. It would've looked worse for me to refuse to go."

He was thinking that over, when I added: "If we had turned against you, we could have given you away. We could have pulled you out of the wagon and handed you over, but we didn't, did we?"

That made him really think, though his lip still quivered. "That's a fact, you didn't, missus. But . . . but I'm still just a kid, and I don't always understand stuff."

In spite of the fact that he'd shot a man, his childish confusion was real. He was a little boy who'd been through hell. I reached for my handkerchief and handed it to him. "Wipe your face. Then we'll see about lunch. Afterwards we'll put our heads together and figure what to do. All right?"

He nodded again. "I never got breakfast."

Lawrence muttered something under his

breath, but I couldn't make it out. It sounded like a stream of cuss words, and who could blame him? The day had begun under a cloud, and we both suspected there would be others like it before we'd finished whatever it was we were going to do.

Lawrence had always had a good team of men working with him, men who shared his vision and his scholarship and who had joined him because of his high reputation in his field, and I was happy to see that Dan de Vries and Scott Landers were back again.

They had put together a lunch of sorts — beans from the previous night, bacon, and coffee, such as it was.

Dan took care of Jacky first, then handed me a plate with an apology. "It's not much, Sidra, but it's the best we could do. And you can blame Hugh for it."

He pointed his thumb at a young man I hadn't met, then introduced Hugh Stiles who blushed at being the object of Dan's teasing.

"I'm not much of a cook, Missus Givens."

That was obvious, but he was pleasant and very much in earnest.

"It's fine," I said. "But now that I'm here, you don't have to worry. I'll sling the hash.

I'd do it as a matter of survival, but I like to cook."

"Wait'll you taste Sidra's pies," Dan said. "You'll propose on the spot."

Hugh blushed more deeply, and I felt sorry for him, but not too sorry. He looked as though he liked the attention.

"You'll get used to being teased," I told him. "And you know I'm a widow, and they're dangerous. I might just propose to you."

At that he ducked his head and blushed even redder, but he still grinned. I would learn that he might be bashful, but was far from a sissy.

I'd missed the easy banter, the companionship that had evolved between me and these men, even when Edward was alive. We were all dedicated to our work, but friendship and laughter made the long summers, the physical labor, a pleasure. And now I was finding laughter a release from the horrors of the past days.

Hugh must have thought he was expected to say something to be polite, but all he could manage was to stammer: "I . . . I. . . ."

"Never mind me, Hugh," I said. "Sit down and eat and meet Jacky Chastain who obviously isn't waiting for us."

Jacky, I was glad to see, was eating with

the appetite of a healthy ten-year-old. No worries on that score at least! He was on his second helping when the apparition appeared at the edge of camp — a figure from a medieval tomb, bearded, robed, leading a heavily burdened burro that let out a squeal at the sight of our horses.

"Father Stefan!" Jacky jumped to his feet and ran toward the stranger, who caught the boy in his arms as he started sobbing again.

"Old Godbolt had Ma and Pa killed, but I'll get him for it . . . and Fallon, too . . . I swear I will!" Jacky's voice was almost unintelligible.

A few days before, in my innocence, I'd have written off a remark like that from a ten-year-old boy as bluster. Now I wasn't too sure. I had an uncharacteristic thought, which was: *And if he tries, I hope he pulls it off. Somebody will have to if the law is like I've heard around here.*

The stranger looked our way but held the boy close, speaking to him in a low voice. Whatever he said seemed to have a calming effect, because Jacky stopped crying and let the man take his hand.

Lawrence and I got up to greet the visitor who, we realized as he came closer, was a priest.

"Stefan Sestric," he said, holding out a large and callused hand. "I see you have come to my lost city."

"Yours?" Lawrence said with a hint of arrogance, as usual assuming that the digs were his.

The priest smiled, though his eyes belied humor.

"Not mine really. I wish it were. I'd like to put up a mission here like Father Kino. That's just my way of thinking about a place I visit sometimes to clear my head. It was a good place for that once, but it seems that the devil has been at work in Lost River while I was gone."

He looked, I thought, more like an avenging angel than a man of God with his V-shaped, shaggy brows raised above dark eyes that were now cold with anger. But the hand that he placed on Jacky's head was gentle.

"I understand, *Padre.* I felt the same way about this place. Now it's been invaded by the devil in disguise," Lawrence said. "How long has this been going on? I heard nothing of it when I first came here last year."

The priest frowned, thinking back. "The trouble is new. Your devil seemed content just to roost here and run cattle. Then something changed him, I think. The people

55

of Lost River are part of my flock. They had no complaints until Godbolt brought in the gunman, Fallon. Who can say why? I have reported what I know to the archbishop to get his influence to bring in federal investigators. So far nothing has happened." He shrugged. "They won't listen, not even to a priest. Especially not to this priest."

"Why not?" I asked.

"Because they think I am a foolish man who wanders the desert taking pictures of the Indians. Which I do because they are vanishing as we stand here and something of beauty with them. And besides, this parish is big and spread wide, and it is mine. But . . . well, they look on me and my cameras as if I am mad, and perhaps I am. Who can say?"

Lawrence broke in impatiently. "What will happen to these people in the valley if even you and your *bishop* can't get the federal government to step in?" He put a special inflection on bishop that expressed his opinion of religions in general.

The priest shrugged. "We can't expect too much very soon. Look what happened to the Indians. It's happening to my Indians yet. Now it's happening to poor homesteaders for the same reasons. They are squatting on land someone stronger covets. There are few of them and they have no real political organization and almost no money. It's an old story. I can't say what will happen to them if someone doesn't come to their assistance." He sighed and looked away as he said the next words. "They will have to learn to take care of themselves . . . others did . . . over in Lincoln County."

Lawrence had no comeback. It was obvious that the priest was suggesting people take the law into their own hands, an action beyond his understanding or experience.

"Vigilante law always comes when the regular machinery breaks down," I put in. "And there doesn't seem to be any law here at all if even little old grannies are being poisoned."

Jacky interrupted. "Father got there in time to bury Granny. But it was Mercy and Harve that found her."

The face of the hanged man came vividly to mind. "Harve?" I asked.

"Yeah. The sheriff took him away 'cause Harve said Fallon was the one who poisoned her. Fallon had been hangin' around, makin' friends with her, prob'ly hopin' to steal the place."

Lawrence sighed. I could imagine how the New England Brahmin in him was taking all of this. He said: "Before we think about

57

anything, we have Joe's body to bury. It's good to have you here, Father, to do up the service properly."

Stefan nodded. "Of course. Joe was a good man, a good father. Later you can explain what happened."

It occurred to me that he must be hungry. "Have you eaten?"

Stefan smiled again, his face lighting up so that he became, on the instant, a saint instead of avenging angel. "Not since early morning."

"Then come and eat," Lawrence said. "I feel what you must feel in this place. Obviously we have some things in common."

Whatever those things were — and, of course, I knew — religion and the Church wasn't one of them. Lawrence was a complete pagan, a trait I'd always, in some way, admired. He worshipped the sun and moon, Apollo and Diana, the ancient spirits of the Indians whose remains he always left untouched, the mountains that had sheltered them for centuries.

Of Father Stefan, I wasn't sure. There was something in his wildly gentle face that promised surprise. As events proved, I wasn't wrong.

Immediately after lunch, the men went out

to choose a burial site, taking Jacky with them. He showed them his pa's favorite spot, on a gentle slope near a juniper tree, and with all of them at work with shovels and picks it seemed only minutes before they came back for the body.

While they were gone, I'd found a clean canvas in the supply wagon and, praying the old cloth wouldn't open and reveal what I never wanted to see again, I stitched a decent shroud. I thought I'd never get used to the burying of loved ones so far from civilization, in places where no one might ever come again, and with no headstone, however crude, to guard them.

Jacky had said that the bodies claimed by the dead wagon were never found, but were probably in a common grave and covered over without prayer or ceremony. At least we'd saved Joe Chastain that indignity.

Father Stefan read the Prayers for the Dead, then closed his missal with a snap and raised his head. "Joe and Molly Chastain were good and honorable people. Their deaths were unwarranted . . . a crime of the worst sort. I pray that their deaths were not in vain, and that God's justice will be done in this beautiful valley. And I pray for the safety of Sidra and Jacky as I'm sure you all do."

"Amen," I murmured, then walked slowly down the hill, leaving the men to fill the grave.

In camp I busied myself cleaning the wagon and checking my cameras and equipment and then turned to setting the rude camp kitchen to rights. Lawrence always brought along enough basics so no one was forced to leave work to shop for supplies, and I found the usual sacks of flour, sugar, beans, salt, coffee, and potatoes, plus canned goods and a bushel of apples that were beginning to wither.

My ability to cook with whatever was available had been honed by my several years in the field, and I soon had an apple pie ready for baking and was chopping potatoes for a stew.

Jacky had come in and attached himself to me like a mollusk, as if fearing that I, too, would be taken away, and I let him help me with the pie crust and search out whatever utensils had been scattered.

"I bet those were our cows bein' run off," he said as he stood beside me chewing on an apple. "Pa and me brought them up here last week, but they ain't here now."

"You mean they were stolen?"

He gave me a look that pitied my innocence. "That's how it is. They burn us out, steal our cattle. My horse ain't around, either."

Of course, I knew about range wars and rustling. One couldn't live in the West and not hear about such things. "Where can he hide all those cows?" I asked. "The valley isn't big enough to hide everybody's stolen cattle. They'd be found, wouldn't they?"

"He changes brands or runs them across the line. In Mexico nobody cares whose they are. Besides, he owns a ranch down there, too."

I didn't need to ask who "he" was. Instead, I said: "You think your horse is in Mexico, with the cows?"

Jacky choked down a sob. "Maybe. Or maybe I'll find him hangin' around. He prob'ly misses me. I had him since he was a colt."

For once I had no words of comfort. I knew how it felt to lose a loved one, but those things that had been Edward's and mine, though inanimate, had been left to me and were doubly cherished for their memories.

"We'll all keep an eye out," I said. "What does he look like?"

He wiped at his eyes. "His name's Poco, 'cause he's little. And Pa called him a grulla." My face expressed my ignorance, and he added: "That means he's kind of gray. Like a mouse."

Without another word, I reached for a damp towel and blotted his tears. "We'll do our best," I promised. "Now do you think you could rustle me up some wood for the fire?"

"I reckon you must think I'm an awful baby." His words were muffled by the cloth, and all the more heart-rending for it.

"No," I said, bending down. "No. We think you're a very courageous young man, and we're proud to have you here. Now go find me that wood."

I watched as he made his way past the large tents that had been put up, one for dining, two others for cleaning and sorting artifacts, and up the sloping south side of the cañon that was grassy and shaded by oak and juniper. If it was in my power to find his missing horse, I would do it. Any child, but especially Jacky, needed something familiar to love. With a smile I remembered Everett stretching out his arms to the stuffed bear. I had solved that problem, perhaps I would be equally lucky with this one, and perhaps I had something of the mother in me, after all.

After supper, which disappeared faster than I could dish it out, Lawrence gave his usual, semi-formal welcoming speech, with a few additions.

"You all know what happened this morning," he began, "so I won't go over it again. What some of you may not know is that the colonel knows Jacky witnessed the killings, and that Sidra was there, too. It's obvious from what we've seen and heard that the man will stop at nothing. He wants Jacky out of the way, and probably Sidra, because he suspects she knows more than she admitted.

"So we keep both of them here, hide them if necessary, and keep our eyes and ears open. If I didn't need every one of you, I'd post a guard at the cañon entrance. As it is, I want you to stay alert. I wouldn't put it past Godbolt to raid us, too, and at any time. You've all got pistols. Keep them handy. If trouble comes, it'll be the whole crew they're after. Godbolt doesn't like witnesses. Clear?"

From the expressions on the faces of his audience, he'd made himself perfectly clear. Only Dan, the irrepressible, made a joke.

"Just like in a dime novel."

Lawrence wasn't amused. "I can assure you, this isn't a fairy tale. The man plays for keeps."

Dan took the reprimand in stride. Having known Lawrence for years, he was well acquainted with his friend's habits. "Yes, boss," he said, with a wink at me.

Lawrence cleared his throat and went on, this time with a half smile curling his mouth. "In addition to Hugh Stiles, Jacky Chastain will be working with us. He'll be available to help anyone who needs his assistance." He nodded at Jacky, whose mouth had dropped open at the unexpected attention.

"Most of you are familiar with my methods by now, but for Hugh and Jacky, I'll repeat myself. I prefer to work with a small group. I don't hire extra workers, can't on my budget. I'm not simply looking for pottery and baskets to take back to sell or exhibit, and I'm not expecting to dig up the gold of Mycenæ. What I do want is to date the site and find out who these people were and how they lived. No gold-diggers allowed."

Across from me, Stefan was smiling at Lawrence's subtle humor. Coronado and his army had ruined themselves in a vain search for gold and what there was, was being mined by modern methods in tunnels deep beneath the earth. Whoever had lived in this cañon had no interest in the white man's metal. Survival had been their most important task.

"When I was here last summer, I found positive evidence of a large village, possibly a permanent site. We'll know more as we excavate. Sidra as usual will take photos of each step and each artifact. We'll catalogue and describe what we find and pack up the most important pieces for shipment. Barring any more stampedes, we should have a successful summer. Any questions?"

"What one man leaves behind is another's treasure," Stefan said.

Lawrence beamed. "Precisely. You could call us detectives looking for clues left behind a thousand years ago. Who lived here? What did they eat? Hunt? Wear? What gods did they worship?"

Jacky tugged at my arm. "What's My . . . Myceenee?"

"It's a very, very old city in Greece. Did you learn about Greece in school?"

He frowned, thinking hard. "No, missus. I hardly ever got to go to school. But I can read. And write, too. Ma taught me."

"Well," I said, "sometime, when he's not

65

busy, Doctor Haslett can tell you all about Greece and Mycenæ. Or you could ask Father Stefan."

Jacky's eyes were drooping, and who could blame him? Ancient Greece and education would have to wait. "Let's get you to bed," I said.

Once again he looked miserable and frightened. "Where'm I supposed to sleep?"

I took his hand. "There's an extra cot in my wagon. Will that be all right?"

"I guess."

He dropped into bed as soon as I had it made up and was asleep as soon as his head was on the pillow.

CHAPTER EIGHT

Breakfast was over and Lawrence and the crew were busy marking the boundaries of the first unit to be excavated. Jacky was washing dishes, which he was doing with a great clatter, partly to conceal an occasional sob.

With Stefan's help I was setting up the small tent I used for developing. He had heard about the Eastman roll film and the new glass plates pre-prepared with developing emulsion, and was curious about the process. I'd shown him the vats, the developing fluid, the stop bath I'd brought with me, along with fixative and distilled water, as I never knew what the water in the field would contain. Charles Lummis, in his photographs of the New Mexico Indians, had used water from the Río Grande, and, as a result, many of his photographs had turned blue, a disaster I hoped to avoid. Somehow, though, our talk had turned from science to people. As I was discovering, Stefan was a person who was capable of thinking about and analyzing several things at once.

"In my country," he went on, "there are still some who believe in werewolves and witches as an explanation of evil. Not so different from the native people here. And who can say there aren't those possessed by the devil?"

"If greed is the same thing as being possessed, I won't argue," I said. "Godbolt wants to own the whole valley, maybe the whole territory, and it looks like he won't stop until he does. But what for? In the long run, I mean?"

"Perhaps he thinks he's God."

"That's crazy!"

Stefan hammered in the last tent peg, then sat down, folding his robes around him. "There's little difference between obsession and being possessed, Sidra. Most wars have started with one man's obsession."

"Is this a war, then?" I sat beside him.

"Of course. War is one of man's favorite games, if you stop to think. Here in the West you've had many. Small ones, and many before our time, but a part of history."

I had never seen myself as involved in what would be written, only in what could be seen. Life had been, before now, so simple.

"I'm not sure I like being part of history. This part, anyhow," I said.

"Like it or not, you're involved." He pointed to Jacky and then to the camera. "If only because of them."

For that, I had no answer. But later, when I'd developed the film, when the horror of the previous morning was reproduced for us to see, I knew I couldn't remain a bystander, silent and giving approval by that silence.

"Tomorrow I'll go down and see if there is anything left of Molly," Stefan said, his face both saddened and angry. "You keep the boy with you."

"You have more courage than I do."

He shook his head. "We do what we must, Sidra. And she was a fine woman."

"I hate it here!" The words burst out

before I could stop them, and they were true. It was as if I'd stumbled into a nightmare that had no beginning and no end.

He reached out and put his hands on my shoulders, and for one moment I thought he was going to pull me into an embrace — an embrace I, to my shame, would have welcomed, but he stepped away quickly as if he, too, had been burned. "You don't hate it. You have your work. Do it. And let the land give you peace."

I wasn't sure I'd ever find peace again, particularly not when my own body had responded to his touch, but I answered as calmly as I could. "I'll try. And God bless you."

He chuckled. "That's for me to say." Then he turned and walked away, his robes swirling around him, his feet kicking up small puffs of dust.

While Stefan was gone on his errand of mercy, I went to work developing some of his photographs, taking great care with the plates which, he told me, he carried himself in a heavy case, instead of entrusting them to the burro.

"He's sure-footed, but I'd rather not blame him in an accident," he'd said, handing me the box.

"But you'll trust me with them?"

"Of course."

What I expected to find, I don't know, but as the images came clear, I saw that Stefan not only had mastered a technique, he was blessed with an eye for subject and for composition. Obviously he knew what he was after and got it — a Navajo mother, her arms curved around her child, a dark Renaissance Madonna; children herding sheep, silhouetted sharply against a white mesa; an old woman weaving a basket, closely watched by two young girls; a ceremonial dance, the dancers masked, caught in a blur of motion. And in all of them I saw his love of humanity, a reverence, not only for his subjects, but for the land and for life.

What I held in my hands was treasure, a record of a vanishing culture. Compared to his achievement, my landscapes, my few studies of Lizzie Roanhorse, seemed pale, puny, lacking direction. And I'd dared to call myself a photographer!

I was sunk in self-pity when Stefan came wearily to the tent. One look at his face, set in sadness, kept me from talking about my doubts.

"You found her?"

He sighed, and sat down. "If that's what you call it. I buried what there was, blessed the grave, said the prayers, and felt . . . trivial. My prayers came too late."

Although I myself had no strong belief in prayers, either before or after the fact, I reached out and touched his hand. "You don't know that."

"I know nothing." He refused my comfort with a shake of his head. All I have are questions without answers. What good is faith? Can you tell me, Sidra?"

I searched my own life, a series of inner images recalled. At last I said: "It keeps us alive."

"For what?"

"For whatever comes."

He propped his elbows on his knees, put his chin in his hands. "You think so?"

"No," I said, "I hope so."

To my surprise, he laughed, and the lines of sorrow on his face disappeared.

"Thank you," he said. "It's good to laugh. I don't do it enough."

"I guess none of us has laughed much lately. And I was sitting here feeling very sorry for myself."

"Why?"

"Your pictures. They're so perfect. So right. Come see."

Together we went through them and, looking a second time, was like seeing through

71

his eyes. The sharing of a vision happens rarely, if at all, and sitting side-by-side in the hot little tent, I felt that I was holding a fragile, lovely globe of glass in which all life, all thought, all passion was visible, and it was up to me to keep it intact.

I looked once more at the mother and child, saw that Stefan had captured the essence of motherhood — the pride, the never-ending fear for the young, the tenderness.

"This goes beyond photography," I said. "This one is miraculous."

"One out of hundreds. The rest . . . failures." He made a gesture as if to destroy.

"No!" I gathered up the photos and held them close. "You're too harsh a critic. These are . . . are . . . I don't have the words to tell you."

"But they're not what I saw." He gave me a sideways glance. "Oh, don't worry. I'll keep them with the rest at the mission. They're what I'll leave to the world. My children."

Abruptly he went out, shattering the afternoon.

Stefan left us the morning of the party, having stayed longer than he'd intended, primarily, or so he said, because of Jacky.

"The boy needs to be comforted," he said.

"I try, but . . . but it's impossible. Who can comfort such a loss?"

"Keep trying. He loves you, you know."

"Oh," I said, a weak response.

He shot me a sharp look. "You doubt me or the possibility of love?"

Cautiously I examined my feelings, those for Jacky, and those for this strange man who, unintentionally, had brought me back to life. "Maybe both," I said.

"Don't. Love is where you find it, as is God. Accept it and don't argue."

It seemed blasphemous to talk about God and what I called love when, in the short time I'd spent with Stefan, my feelings — woman for man — had strengthened in a manner that frightened me. I had not felt this way even about Edward, and, as a result, shame and desire were at war inside me. With a deftness learned from the master, I changed the subject. "Where you're going now . . . is it far?"

He acknowledged my cowardice with one of his penetrating glances as if he'd read my confusion. "Too far I think sometimes. From here it's five days' travel, but the reservation is part of my parish, if that's what you want to call a thousand miles of desert with a few hundred souls scattered across it. But I'd go even if it wasn't a duty. The journey gives me time to think."

"About what?" I asked, curious. But I'd gotten too close.

He shrugged. "Who can say? For me it's a ritual. Like baptism or the Muslim pilgrimage to Mecca." He was packing the burro, taking care with the bundles that held his precious camera, his vestments, a chalice, a wooden crucifix, and talking in that half cynical way that opened doors in my mind. "When I get there, they'll bring me babies to be baptized. Then they'll ask to be married as if they haven't been together for a year and handed me the squalling result. All this they do to please me, for whatever reason. Because when I'm gone, they go back to what they've always believed. They'll pray to their own gods as well as ours. It makes me wonder what use I am, or why I do what I do."

"Well?" I prompted.

"The idealism of youth still with me maybe."

"But you aren't young," I said. "And life is short."

"You speak from experience?" His eyes under those heavy brows were laughing.

"Don't make fun. All I've seen lately is dying and death and broken dreams, and

74

I'm tired of it. So must you be with what you do, though you won't admit it."

He sighed and took my hand between his two big ones. "Sidra, I could tell you to offer your sorrow to God. I could say all the words that are meaningless, to me as well as to you, but I won't. Time changes things. And people. You have much to do here. Think of that and do your best."

"I want to stop time!" I cried. "I want to keep what I see. I want what was." That was as close as I'd ever come to speaking the truth, and he understood. But as was his way, he offered argument.

"At what point would you stop it? And for how long? If you did, you'd upset a fine balance. As it is, you catch moments with pictures, and being able to make a vision tangible is a gift from God. Don't ask for more."

"So I'm greedy like the rest. I can't help it." I kicked at a pebble, wishing I'd never started the conversation.

"There's a difference between passion and greed. It's up to you to find out what it is." He patted my hand. "I'll be back in two weeks, and we can continue this. By then I'll be tired of preaching and praying."

That surprised me. "You're not supposed to admit it."

"No. But I'm human as well as being a priest." He picked up the burro's lead rope. "Keep safe, Sidra. And keep Jacky safe. Perhaps things will be better by the time I come back."

I watched as he headed down the cañon and disappeared around the bend.

He hadn't been gone over an hour during which I puttered around camp, sorely missing him, when Lawrence called to me as he approached from up the hill.

In one of the caves in the north cliff high above us, he had found the remains of a young woman whose skull had recently been bashed in.

CHAPTER NINE

We stood inside the mouth of the cave staring down at what had been human only a few months before. Whoever had killed her had packed the body here from somewhere else, perhaps only from the ledge outside. There were drag marks inside the cave in the dirt floor, but none outside where the wind whipped the rock shelf bare. The killer had obviously never envisioned anyone coming to this remote spot for years, perhaps centuries. They had made no effort to drag the body deep inside. *Perhaps, also,* I thought, *they weren't strong enough to drag the body far. But who would that be? Even Jacky is strong as an ox for his age.* I kept my thoughts to myself.

The girl lay crumpled in a heap, what remained of her clothes in shreds, her flesh half eaten. My stomach heaved, and I turned away, stumbling out into the light.

"Who . . . ?" I began, but couldn't go on.

"Whether the sheriff's Godbolt's man or not, we have to report this." Lawrence came to stand beside me. "It may or may not have anything to do with the rest of the killings. I'm going to town. You stay here and don't say anything. Especially not to Jacky."

He didn't have to worry. Any words I had were useless to describe what I'd seen. And I'd seen something Lawrence had overlooked. A second partially deteriorated form farther inside the dark interior, that of a small child.

"This place is cursed," I said as we scrambled down the steep path. "It's no wonder whoever lived here before disappeared. We'll be lucky to get out ourselves."

Lawrence looked at me, annoyed. "Calm down. It's true that some places are inherently evil. I've been in them. But this isn't one. All of this is connected in some way to

Godbolt. We just have to find the thread."

"And hope he lets us live long enough!"

"Are you trying to tell me you quit?" he asked. "I never saw you as a quitter."

Was I? I took a deep breath, then another. Leaving would mean abandoning Jacky and interrupting serious work, all because I'd lost courage. It would also mean that I might never see Stefan again.

Stop that! I scolded myself. Not the least of the evil was the fact that I found myself attracted to a priest.

"Of course, I'm not quitting," I said. "It's just that . . . seeing her up there after all that's happened . . . well, it got to me. I feel like I'm fighting shadows. Like any minute I'll get a bullet in the back."

Lawrence picked up a bridle and walked toward his horse in the little corral. "Life's a funny thing, but we keep going. What else have we? Now do what I said and I'll be back as soon as I can. I'm counting on you."

Everyone was counting on me — Sidra Givens, widow, photographer, would-be artist, woman lost in a maze. "I'll be here," I said.

"Trig Cassidy," the deputy said to me without bothering to remove his hat. "You found the body?"

78

"Doctor Haslett did," I corrected.

"Any idea who it is?"

Lawrence interrupted him. "Certainly not. As I told you and the sheriff, we're not here to investigate murders. Go and see the remains for yourself."

"How come you know it's a murder?" Cassidy asked, and his voice revealed what he was thinking: that Lawrence had let it slip out.

"Go look for yourself. Anybody but an idiot can tell that. You'll see how her head is twisted, practically pulled loose from her neck. Somebody probably strangled her, and she tried to fight them off. Besides, you're obviously suspicious of the wrong people. We've new here and that body must have been there for at least a month."

Not happy over the messy job he knew was facing him, the deputy went up the path and into the cave. When he came down again, he was white-faced and grim. "You were right. It's a murder. Somebody killed her. Probably the kid, too, but I don't see any signs of how he got it. You got a blanket or a canvas I can wrap the bodies in? They'll probably fall apart if we try to drag them. Besides, I don't get paid enough to handle dead ones. I've got a notion to leave them there for the coroner."

In what was, for him, an unnaturally calm voice, Lawrence said: "Kid? What kid? What the hell are you talking about?"

I recognized the symptoms of one of his fits of temper coming on as they always did when he got an unhappy surprise. His voice got higher with each word. Lawrence could be a really funny example of consternation when he felt he'd lost control of a situation.

I stepped up and laid a hand on his arm. "It's true. There was another decomposed little body. A . . . a child's. I didn't say anything because I knew you'd be even more upset about the whole thing . . . and I guess because it was just too awful. I was in shock for a while."

Ordinarily when Lawrence was angry, I could see the funny side, but this was different.

"Thank you," he said in a level, deadly voice, "for protecting me from the truth. Are you telling me that whoever killed that woman murdered a baby, too?"

"Yes," I said. "At least that's how it looked. Or else the child could have died from neglect later. Either way, it's upsetting." And then I had a worse thought, which I kept to myself. *Suppose the infant wasn't killed but had starved to death?*

At that, I started crying, unable to control

80

myself any longer. It was all too much. Lawrence's mood changed at once. He moved close and put his arms around me. "I'm sorry," was all he said.

Even the deputy didn't horn in, but stood by awkwardly until I finally turned around, still drying my eyes.

With a frown, Lawrence said: "It makes sense to send for the coroner. Unless we find out who she is, it might be as well to simply bury her up here." He was back in control, and no more anxious than the deputy to touch the bodies. "I'll go hunt up a canvas to cover them, though. No sense in letting the coyotes gnaw them another night."

He went off to find a canvas and the deputy rolled a cigarette and lit it. Then he surprised me by saying: "I'm sorry, ma'am. You must be havin' a pretty terrible time. Bein' new here and all."

"Terrible time isn't the half of it," I said. "I wish I'd never come here."

His next words astonished me. "So do I . . . I mean I wish I'd never come here. Lincoln County in the old days was bad enough. But they never killed women and babies."

I'd had enough of dead bodies. Leaving the men to cover them up, I went down to where I'd hidden Jacky in my photo-developing tent. He was sorting photographs, and looked up with a scowl.

"What's *he* doin' here?" he asked.

I told him and was touched by the misery in his eyes. "A little kid?" he asked to be assured he'd heard right. "Who'd kill a baby?" Then after a long silence he said miserably: "I wish Ma was still alive."

Who could blame him? For his question, I had no answer. I simply opened my arms and let him burrow against me, lost child in a world that should have been simple but which even I couldn't fathom — lost woman that I was.

I went back outside and found Lawrence and Cassidy talking. Cassidy said: "The coroner won't be up here tomorrow, and maybe not till the next day, knowin' old Doc Goldwater. I might as well go back to town. Maybe I can prod him a little."

"You do that," Lawrence said.

I kept Jacky under cover until Cassidy left. When it was safe for him to come out, I reminded him of our invitation. "Mister Haslett and I are going over to Godbolt's ranch like we promised." I hoped that didn't re-arouse his suspicions about us. To avert that, I added: "I need the money for taking the pictures, now that I have a family."

"Family?"

"You," I said. "The only family I've got any more."

He turned that over in his boy's head, and finally smiled. He said: "Does that mean that, when we know each other better, I can call you ma?"

I knelt and hugged him close, little brave, bony figure, little lost boy. "You can start calling me ma right now."

"Can I?"

"Of course."

"OK, Ma," he said, then noticed my tears. "How come you're crying? Did I say something wrong?"

"No," I told him. "You said something right. Very right. I always wanted a boy of my own."

Lawrence who had been watching and listening turned away and walked off, saying over his shoulder: "I'm going to get on a fresh shirt for the colonel's shindig." I wondered if he wasn't avoiding having us see his eyes. Men aren't supposed to cry. Especially unemotional scientists.

As we pulled away in the buckboard with my bulky camera equipment stowed behind the seat, Jacky waved, and, if I'm not mistaken, called after us: "Good bye, Ma."

Good bye, Son, I said to myself, since we

were too far away for him to hear, and what I was feeling was still too fresh to explain to Lawrence.

I hoped Jacky would stay out of sight as much as possible. Godbolt was bound to set a watch on our camp sooner or later, if he hadn't already.

CHAPTER TEN

Godbolt's *hacienda* was surrounded by a high stone wall. He had planned carefully and built a self-sustaining, defensible fort. Enclosed by the wall were the main house, stables, and corrals well back behind the house, screened from it by cottonwoods, a bunkhouse behind the corrals, two deep wells — one in the courtyard of the main house and another by the corral — and an orchard and gardens. Heavy, carved wooden gates guarded the entrance.

That night they stood open to admit a stream of riders, buckboards, and carriages — the cream of Lost River society. The poorer folks who came in wagons, and there were a few, the nesters who'd sold out to Godbolt and worked for him, had to leave their rude conveyances outside the walls.

Lanterns hung from every branch and lined the drive that led to the house. Their effect completely clashed with the idea of fortifications, nor were they what I would have expected from a man like the colonel.

The main house, too, was a surprise. It was territorial-style with the customary deep, vine-covered portal, and it seemed, at first sight at least, to be a place of warmth and welcome. Guests were wandering in a carefree manner on the paths surrounding the house. Although there was war in this land, and it lay at the door of the master of this *hacienda,* all was peace here, and I thought: *When will the guns begin to shoot?* I wasn't going to have long to wait, but for the time enjoyed the atmosphere, especially the music of a guitar and violin coming from somewhere unseen, sweet as birdsong or the water that trickled out of a small fountain.

A servant held our horses' heads while Lawrence helped me down and reached for my camera and equipment.

"Is this real?" I whispered.

"Real as a solid gold brick. There's no doubt money built the place."

I couldn't help but gawk at the women in their sumptuous party dresses of silk and lace and velvet, at their display of jewels, and at their shoes — mostly dainty kid slippers with buckles and rosettes peeping out from under swirling skirts — unlike the sturdy leather boots which were all I'd brought with me.

"I feel like kitchen help," I muttered.

Lawrence was never one to let me undervalue myself. "You've got more brains in your little finger than the whole bag of them have in their heads. Remember that. Besides, modesty doesn't become you. You're the prettiest woman here, whether you know it or not."

I looked him over for some evidence of humor and could see none. "You haven't even been at the punch bowl yet," I said.

"Not yet, but if you don't know you're a lovely woman, I'm not going to tell you again."

I was about to say something — probably dumb — when he cut me off. "Here comes our host. Smile, Sidra. He's no richer than you in the things that count, and this vulgar display isn't one of them."

I hoped the colonel didn't hear him, since he hadn't bothered to lower his voice. Arrogance was Lawrence's birthright, and so was money, but neither was mine. I did, however, manage a smile.

With the colonel, business came before pleasantries. "Here you are at last. We'll get the picture-taking over with. Then you'll be free to enjoy the party."

He motioned to a servant to carry my equipment and led the way into the *zaguán,* the center hall of the house. At the far end stood a young girl whose beauty, even at a distance, was astonishing. Lawrence whistled under his breath, and this time Godbolt heard but didn't seem to mind. In fact he came as close to beaming as I imagine it was possible for him.

"Her mother would have been proud," he said, pointing to a portrait that hung above a heavy, Spanish-Colonial chest.

It was easy to see the resemblance between mother and daughter. Both were fair-haired and perfect of feature, and both possessed eyes of a deep, almost purple blue, the color of an iris. I wondered why a woman such as that had married a man like Godbolt, then answered myself. For money, of course — or the power that money meant. Could there be any other reason? Certainly not love!

The colonel led us to Celine, and she watched us without moving, like a queen waiting to be approached. I thought: *I'll be damned if I'll curtsy, and I'm sure Lawrence won't!*

"Allow me to present my daughter, Celine," Godbolt said.

It was a wonder he didn't do it the other way around and present us to her highness, who ignored me and extended her hand to Lawrence. In her way, she was very Latin. For her, only men existed. Women were merely a nuisance to be relegated to the background or gotten rid of as soon as possible.

Up close, she was, if possible, even lovelier, with an innocence that I found remarkable, considering who she was. If it was an act, it was an incredibly good one I decided after we'd been introduced.

Finally she turned to me with a smile and said in a small, affected voice that I was sure she'd practiced: "I've never been photographed like this before. You'll have to tell me what to do."

I did a little affectation myself, sounding brusque and business-like, as though she was the parlor maid. "Be yourself. Keep still, but don't freeze and look unnatural if you can help it. A lot of people do, and they come out looking mad at the world. Maybe they are," I added.

"I'm not."

"Why should you be? Especially tonight."

"Daddy says he promised Mummy this a long time ago. And this summer he's sending me to Europe." She looked expectant, like a kid invited to an ice cream parlor for the first time. She said: "I've never been anywhere really. Just here and in Mexico where Daddy's mines are."

Mines . . . Mexico, I thought, *that explains one source of this opulence.* I suspected there were others — railroads, stocks, cattle — that I'd discover if I let the girl chatter, but doubted she could shed any light on what had made her father into a monster. As Stefan had said, the man thought he was God, and was doing his best to prove it.

While we talked, I was busy setting up the tripod and the heavy 8 × 10 camera. Eastman's film was fine for some work, but for this I preferred the big glass plates that, with their detail, captured light, shadow, nuance, absorbing all and giving it back with absolute clarity beyond the eye's capability to distinguish.

The *zaguán* was brilliantly lit with candles in silver wall sconces and in heavy, silver chandeliers, but I'd brought my flash pan to make certain. I posed Celine in a carved, high-backed chair, a foil for her yellow hair, her slim, white lace gown. She was an obedient subject, remaining motionless except for a sudden blush and a widening of her eyes as I took the last shot. What had she seen that caused such a reaction?

89

I ducked out from under the black silk drapery and came face to face with Nash Fallon, who, like the girl, was even more handsome up close than from a distance, with high cheek bones, a slash of dark brows, and beneath them eyes the blue of midnight.

"Nash." It was almost a whisper, but he turned quickly, inclined slightly from the waist to Celine, and gave her a smile that wasn't quite the kind I'd have expected from a lover. I have no idea why I thought that, or even watched closely enough to notice it. But I'd found him fascinating from the first time I'd laid eyes on him, just as most women did. I suspected he was used to it.

Lust, love, or simply the attraction between a pair of young and beautiful animals, these two, in this time at least, belonged together. I wanted to ask them both to sit for me, but I recognized that Fallon, for some reason, was impatient.

"Are you finished here?" he asked Celine curtly.

She looked at me, and I nodded.

"When can I see the pictures?" she wanted to know.

"I'll bring them in a day or two."

She remembered her manners then. "Mis-

90

sus Givens, this is Nash Fallon. He's a friend of Daddy's."

Friend, I thought. *What a strange, incongruous choice of words.*

Handsome he was, but I didn't like him. "I saw you at the hanging," I said.

His face didn't change. Undoubtedly he was a very good poker player. His kind never give anything away.

"Hanging?" Celine looked first at me, then at Nash.

Fallon ignored her and said to me in a flat voice: "The man got what he deserved. He poisoned a little old lady."

His eyes, in spite of their depth of color, were expressionless. *Did the man feel anything at all?* I wondered. *Or had the ability to feel been destroyed in him, perhaps never even present? If that were so, then he was as much a monster as Godbolt, lacking a soul, or any semblance of humanity. Regardless of that, he had a face a master painter would have loved.*

The taste of anger is thick and black — like tar. It clogs the throat, blots out politeness and common sense. Only too clearly I saw Harve's face, tongue out in death, hanging from a rope, and the stark sorrow of his wife. I saw Joe Chastain's blood on this man's hands, and Jacky's irreconcilable

91

grief. With that in the forefront of my mind, I spoke without regard for company or courtesy to my hostess.

"I heard there were two murders. Granny Prosser's and Harve's, since he didn't do it."

Fallon must have realized that I'd been told he was the principal suspect among all but his own crowd, and his lip curled as if he thought I was a fool.

"You shouldn't believe everything you hear. We've had trouble with nesters in the valley, and the man you saw was a ring-leader. But as you see, his kind are taken care of. You don't need to concern yourself. Or you either, Celine," he said to the girl who was listening intently.

Though he spoke like a gentleman, with a slight Texas drawl, he was warning me subtly to mind my own business.

"Murder, or however you want to disguise it . . . seems to be an epidemic here," I said. "First the hanging, then the Chastains are burned out and killed . . . it seems there's no law, no decency in this place!" *There!* I thought. *Let them chew on that a while!*

Just for a second, Celine's face hardened, and another girl looked out at me from her narrowed eyes. Then she stamped her foot. "I don't want to talk about it!" she cried.

"This is a party. *My* party. You promised to dance with me, not to stand here talking about dead people nobody cares a fig for."

With a smile, he took her arm. "I did, and I will."

I wanted to take that beautiful child aside and warn her that her life was balanced on a precipice, that the man she loved didn't exist except in her dreams — and that at least some of the dead had also been much loved. A foolish desire, but, in any case, I never got the chance.

Without warning, a spatter of bullets swept the portal, followed by the crash of guns and the sound of running feet. Women were screaming, and the pounding of hoofs drowned out any concerns I may have had about Celine. Instead, I thought of Godbolt's words. "The nesters are organizing against me." Little did he know.

CHAPTER ELEVEN

"In here! And stay away from the window!" Lawrence appeared out of nowhere and dragged me into one of the rooms, a library I supposed, seeing the paneled bookcases that reached to the ceiling.

In spite of his warning, he was looking out. "It looks like the local folks have had enough. While you were busy, I met the sheriff, Judge Crandall, and the mayor, all gathered together in one place. Just right for an ambush."

I huddled in the folds of heavy velvet draperies wishing I'd brought my pistol. At the last minute I'd decided against taking it in the house and stowed it under the wagon seat. *Never again,* I promised myself. From that moment, wherever I went, my .41 went, too.

Lawrence drew a small Derringer out of his boot. "I wasn't about to come in here unprepared," he bragged, and I refrained from making a derisive comment about his choice of weapon.

"Where'd you get that?" I asked, instead.

He laughed. "A gentleman's always prepared, but my Forty-Five's too big to wear to a party. You can be sure, though, that I wasn't about to come here defenseless."

At that moment, a bullet crashed through the window and buried itself in the paneling on the far wall.

"Get down!" I hissed. "For God's sake!"

"God has nothing to do with it." He sat, but there was a gleam in his eye.

"You're enjoying this," I said, recalling Stefan's theory about men and war.

"It's certainly different."

In the *zaguán,* a woman screamed, and Lawrence edged toward the door, crouching low. A moment later he was back, leading Celine, her face a study, not of fear but of rage, her hair fallen out of its careful chignon.

"Who is it?" she cried. "Who's doing this? My party . . . it's ruined. And Nash is out there."

She sat beside me, rag doll, perplexed child, about to cry, and I saw my life consumed by having to mother a series of orphans, all of them struggling to comprehend the world and its evils.

"Hush!" I said. "Don't cry. You'll mess your face."

She turned to me, her mouth a tight line. "What's the difference? It's all been spoiled."

And so are you. I didn't say the words, because I saw suddenly that, though true, they were of no use to her.

Outside, the gunfire had ceased, at least for the moment, and the sound of galloping horses faded into the distance leaving behind a silence thick and dark as the bottom of a well.

Celine scrambled to her feet and peered out, but I pulled her back. "Stay down until we're sure it's safe," I warned.

"Something's burning." The fire was reflected in her eyes, an obscene flickering that changed her from child to fury. "It's the bunkhouse and the barn. How dare they? How dare they just come in here and do this? And to us!"

Maybe because you've done it to them, I thought, but kept silent as the yard and the room were lit by dancing flames. I got up, ready to run if the house caught fire. Just then, a stray bullet seemed preferable to immolation.

"I hate them," Celine said in a voice quite different from her earlier, affected one. "It's those nesters, and they'll pay. Daddy and Nash will make sure of that."

So, the cub was like her father. I shivered, though the room was warm. Only a short while before I had thought her an innocent, but once again was struck by duality, by the fact that many of us wear masks.

Outside, I could see a bucket brigade and servants with sacks and shovels beating at the flames, sending sparks flying in all directions. And then, out of the orange glare came Godbolt's riders, Nash Fallon in the lead, his face hidden in the shadow cast by his hat. They galloped down the drive and vanished, an image seen, then gone, photographed by the eye alone.

"They'll get them." Celine's mouth was a straight slash across her white face. "Nash will know what to do."

"What?" I asked.

She laughed. "They'll hang. Or he'll shoot them. But I won't be allowed to watch, even if they did ruin everything. I'm never allowed to watch the hangings. I'm not even supposed to know about them, but I do. I know a lot of things. Secrets."

"You wouldn't want to see," I told her. "Believe me."

She shrugged. "I might."

The front door banged, loud as a gunshot.

"Celine!" The colonel's voice was high and strained.

At the sound of her name she ran, child once more, into her father's arms.

Lawrence shoved the Derringer back in his pocket. "Quite a scene, wasn't it?"

I felt the strength go out of me. "Let's get out of here," I said. "Let's go home."

CHAPTER TWELVE

Morning came slowly in the cañon, the sky brightened, the rock walls took on the color of day, their crevices and turnings gradually revealed as the sun rose higher. For me, always, there was a joy that welled up as I watched the dawn come — as if the world had been created anew and I was its only witness, the first to hear the mournful calling of doves, the first to see leaf patterns against sky, to be touched by the flaming wands of an ocotillo that had, in a stubborn quest for life, grown out of a crack in the rock.

Like those who had lived here before me, I lifted my face to the sun and gave thanks, and the events of the night before seemed far away, the pathetic actions of a people that had nothing to do with the past, with me, or with the glory of the dawn.

For a moment I imagined Stefan, a solitary figure in a grassy plain, singing his own praises to the morning. And then I chastised myself for permitting thoughts of him.

Wicked, I said. *Fallen woman.* We had seen and had talked about evil, horrified at its consequences, yet here I was, desiring the embrace of a man of God — perhaps not in the same class as the evil around us, but sinful just the same.

Abruptly I turned away, poured water into the basin, and washed my face — ritual of purification. The irony of life, its turnings and complexities, made me smile as I stepped outside ready to begin the day's chores.

It had been well after midnight when Lawrence and I drove into camp the night before. As a result, I'd slept later than usual, and the men were up and at work excavating near the long, partially exposed wall that Lawrence thought might have been a pit house or a ceremonial meeting place. He based his opinion partly on the length of the remaining structure and partly because of location — on a small rise that gave a clear view of what had been the village and down the cañon.

The initial problem was that, over centuries, floods had swept through and deposited layer upon layer of alluvial soil over the original floor. Unlike many in those early years, Lawrence preferred to work with only his small, hand-picked team, digging inch by inch into the past and missing nothing, whereas some simply dug up and removed what might have been a treasure trove without thought or care.

Lawrence's way was slow, dirty work — the careful removal of years with trowels and small spades, even teaspoons, the sifting of earth through mesh sieves looking, always, for the most minute clue — a bead, a shard of pottery, a finely chiseled arrowhead or tool, seeds, *metates,* even pieces of bone — anything that would give a clue to the past — and the carting away of soil, a menial task everyone hated.

Earlier, Jacky had been assigned to wheelbarrow duty, but then Lawrence had taken pity on him and put him to work with his own sifter and bucket. He was obviously taking the job seriously, peering into the clumps of earth, the fine sand, like a fortune-teller into tea leaves.

"We promised him a penny for any artifact he finds." Lawrence came up and handed me a cup of coffee.

I took a sip, tried not to gag. "Who made this?"

"Yours truly. It *is* awful, isn't it?"

I emptied the cup and watched the dry soil absorb the contents. "Tomorrow," I said, "tomorrow I'll be up early and make something drinkable. That's a promise. Right now I'm going to develop Celine's plates. The sooner they're done and out of here . . . the sooner we have nothing to do with those people . . . the better I'll like it."

He watched the men at work for a minute before answering. When he did, he was frowning. "I didn't tell you on the way home . . . how could you fall asleep after all the excitement? . . . but those men I met last night . . . Sheriff Briscoe, the judge . . . they're all in it together, or so I gathered."

"In what?" I asked. "Mass murder?"

"That's about it. Something to do with a railroad spur coming through. They're all big stockholders, and they'll benefit two ways if it comes, especially if they own the valley. With the small farmers and ranchers driven out, they have a license to steal."

"Well, hell!" I said as his words sank in. "It's true then. Godbolt's after the whole place, and won't stop till he gets it. But what's he want it for? He's got more money than God."

Neither of us was practical enough to ask why a railroad would build a spur into the Lost River Valley. True there were gold and silver mines farther to the south, but only on a small scale. In the end, too late, we learned that much of the area was underlain by a vast, commercial-grade coal field, enough coal to fuel all the railroads in the West. It was a secret Godbolt had shared with no one, not even his cohorts.

In answer to my question, Lawrence shrugged. "It's got to be more than land and cattle, but I can't figure it. I'm going to send a few telegrams. Duff Henley's the marshal up at Santa Fé and he's a friend of mine. There's also a few congressmen back East who'd be interested in the railroad angle."

101

Knowing a little of his family background, I wondered if what he meant was that the congressmen would be interested in an obscure western railroad project only to get his family's financial backing in the next election — or the one after that, and maybe a lot more. Among other things, his family had made a fortune in saws and files. Eventually they got into importing tin, and finally into copper mines all over the world.

I was thinking clearly about what he proposed to do. "Don't send any messages from Lost River. Go on over to Sacaton. That way you can make sure they get sent."

He looked at me, startled. "You think like a man."

"It's common sense."

"Yes, and common sense isn't common at all. In either sex. I'll leave after lunch."

"Be careful."

"You can count on that." He grinned. "Nobody ever said archaeology would be like this. Except maybe in some Egyptian tomb with a curse on it."

I sighed. "Nobody ever told me my life would be like this, either. Dead bodies, orphans, shoot-outs, and barn burnings. Next time you discover a site, leave me out."

"Adventure is broadening, Sidra," he said. "Think of the stories you can tell your grandchildren."

It was an unfortunate statement. I sighed again. "If I live to have any."

CHAPTER THIRTEEN

The horse came up the cañon at a fast trot.

"Now what?" As usual I was talking to myself in the gloom of the small tent where I was working on the last proof print, a process that was always tricky and doubly so in the field. It involved bolting both plate and photosensitive paper into a frame and then exposing the whole to the sunlight for roughly five minutes. Then I'd go back to the tent, put the print into the stop bath and fixer, and hang to dry. At this point I'd cross my fingers and pray no dust or flying insect would stick to the print and ruin a day's work.

I heard Hugh's voice, then a woman's high-pitched one. Celine's.

"Damn it," I muttered. I wasn't finished, and she'd probably hang around waiting, making me feel rushed. And where was Jacky?

"Sidra." Hugh Stiles spoke hesitantly from outside. He was still one of the shyest men I'd ever met, blushing easily, falling for the silly teasing of the others. Mischief prompted my next words.

"Why don't you show Miss Godbolt around? I won't be too long, and I'm sure she'd be interested in what you're doing."

He cleared his throat. "I. . . ."

"Oh, go on, Hugh. I'll be out quick as I can." And in a lower voice added: "You might make sure Jacky's out of sight."

"He took off soon as he heard her coming."

"Good." That was one less thing to worry about. "Now go be nice, Hugh." I swallowed a chuckle, picturing him, red-faced, with the divine Celine clinging to his arm.

His footsteps receded slowly, and I went back to work, hanging the last of the developed prints on a rack to dry.

When I came out a half hour later, Celine was perched on a rock surrounded by all three men, and she was laughing, her head thrown back, her flat-topped riding hat hanging by its cord around her slender neck. So much for dedicated work!

For a moment I had a vision of all the eligible bachelors in Europe following after her like a flock of geese, and I hoped that, when she went abroad, the colonel intended to send an armed guard with her instead of the usual spinster relative or cautious *duenna.* The girl was a honeypot, regardless of parentage or spoiling.

For the first time, I was glad I had no children, particularly not a daughter. My life hadn't equipped me with the ability to guide a girl through adolescence, was, in fact, unorthodox for the time and place. I was a woman in camp with four men, a situation sure to set tongues wagging. So who was I to criticize this glorious creature?

I waved, and she waved back, then slipped off the rock and came toward me, still laughing. Behind her, Dan, Hugh, and Scott glanced guiltily at me and then slipped away to work. I smothered a smile, knowing I'd tease them over supper.

"I couldn't wait," Celine said. "It's all right, isn't it? I mean for me to come?" She sounded a bit breathless, and I thought that being a siren must take a great deal of effort.

"Certainly. But are you supposed to be out riding alone?" I sounded the perennial old maid.

Her laughter rang out again. "I gave old Juan the slip. Riding with him is like riding with a grandmother. Anyhow, it was easy. Everybody's out chasing whoever ruined my party."

She seemed completely unaware that she, too, might be a target.

"You should take care."

A frown marred her happiness for a moment, then she laughed again. "Canela can outrun any horse in the valley."

What a child she still was! A child armed with arrogance, wealth, and that conflict between innocence and a dawning worldliness I'd seen so plainly the night before.

"Come, see your photographs," was all I said.

They had turned out well. How could they not? Her face was made for photography, and the dark, high-backed chair in which she'd posed only emphasized her delicate bone structure, her fair hair, her haughty and determined chin.

She, of course, was delighted. "It's really me!" she exclaimed, holding the pictures first at arm's length, then closer so she could peer at herself as if in a mirror. "I can have them all, can't I?"

"Of course. They're yours."

"Daddy was going to pay you, but I bet he forgot last night." She reached into a pocket of her skirt and pulled out a handful of bills.

"After what happened, I can't blame him," I said. "But keep your money. I'm sure he'll see that I'm paid."

She set her chin. "No. I'll do it. They're

mine, after all. Now I'd better start back or I'll get scolded for ditching Juan." She thrust the money into my hand, then turned and whistled for her horse that came at a trot.

From one of the saddlebags, she brought out a finely bound leather folder. "See. I thought of everything." She slipped the photographs inside.

"Did you bring a pistol?" I asked, still worried.

"Nobody would dare shoot me." In one motion she was astride and looking down, every inch the lady and untouchable. "Daddy would kill anybody who tried."

She wheeled the animal, waved to the men who had once again stopped work to stare, and set off at a gallop. I watched until she was out of sight. She stopped once. I thought maybe she'd seen a deer and was watching the beautiful animal. Then she turned off the trail in the direction she'd been looking. Odd, but it didn't alarm me.

Only then I looked down at the bills she'd left me. Twice, three times I counted them. A hundred dollars! No one I knew had ever been paid that much for a photograph. No girl I knew went riding around the country unarmed, alone, and carrying what was, to many, a small fortune carelessly shoved in a pocket — a month's pay for a miner.

Troubled, I climbed into my wagon and stowed the money in a trunk. "Foolish child," I remember I said. To myself, of course. "Vain, spoiled, lovely, foolish child."

How foolish, we were all to find out. Not one of us ever saw Celine alive again. And if there had been, before, even a small chance of peace in Lost River Valley, it was obliterated that afternoon, replaced by Old Testament vengeance — a bloody holocaust.

CHAPTER FOURTEEN

"Sidra! Come see this. Then get your camera." Lawrence was clearly excited. His grin stretched across his face and showed most of his teeth.

The men had unearthed a bowl entire. It sat where it had been buried, black on white and as perfect as the day it had come out of the fire.

I dropped to my knees beside it, restraining my hands that wanted to explore the smooth symmetry. That there had been someone centuries before me who had been capable of producing things of such beauty filled me with awe and something like compassion, for self, for all those who respond to life and art.

What struck me most about the piece was the absolute detail of the painted bird that seemed ready to rise up and fly from the bottom of the bowl — a quail, with plumed topknot and a merry eye.

Puzzled, I looked at Lawrence. "But this looks like Mimbrés," I said slowly. "How can it be? We're no place near where they lived."

"We'll make a scientist out of you yet. You're right on both counts." He knelt beside me. "What you have to remember is two things. The first is that we've still not got to the bottom strata, so this might have been left here from a later time. Remember, the Mimbrés culture disappeared, lock, stock, and barrel. We don't know where they went or by what route. Maybe they passed by here. Since the bowl isn't killed . . ." — he paused and waited to see if I remembered the Mimbrés practice of putting a hole in the bottom of bowls left at burials, and then went on when I nodded — "they weren't here long enough to bury anybody."

"Well, thank God for that," I said, laughing.

He grinned and continued his lecture that, I reflected, was what he did best. "We don't yet have any idea of the age of this site and won't until we get farther down, see what

109

kind of houses they built, what tools they had, the usual stuff. But the second thing for you to keep in that curious mind of yours is that these people didn't live in isolation. This was possibly a trade route, and we might find anything . . . abalone or shells from the Sea of Cortéz or the Pacific, parrot feathers from Mexico, clay pipes from the north. There was a city here, though it's hard to imagine. And there were people in it who moved around, possibly with the seasons, traded for what they liked or didn't have. Think of ancient Rome and all the cultures before. The roads leading in and out. *People,* Sidra. People like us. That's what it's all about."

"Surely not Rome," I said, laughing.

"Well, not entirely. The Romans, so I understand, didn't have soap. They bathed without it. Whoever was here probably made soap out of yucca roots. More advanced, don't you think?"

"You're joking. About the soap."

"I'm not. Makes you wonder, doesn't it? How they could stand being packed cheek by jowl into the Colosseum?"

I laughed again. "All those miles of aqueducts, all those ornate baths just to go swimming."

"And other things."

"Like what?" Though I thought I knew, teasing Lawrence was always fun.

He got to his feet. "Get your camera. The light's just right."

"Times have changed," I said, knowing very well that there were some subjects not to be discussed in polite society, not even here, where no such thing as rules existed.

"Not always for the better. Now hurry!"

As I worked, photographing the find from all angles, I was thinking about the history of the world — as I had learned it and as it had been revealed to me through my work.

Stefan had said that we, too, were a part, and I began to understand his meaning. History and culture were people, and the necessities were the same, never changing. Food, shelter, clothing. Having obtained those, people were free to pursue their imagination, some for good, some for evil.

Here, in this isolated cañon, and in other places just as remote, a small Rome had existed, a civilization that had built a center of worship, that appreciated beauty even in the most utilitarian objects. Always, even in the least, there was a reaching out to something other, the need to create with one's own hands, to worship whatever gods had cast their spell.

And I was here, engaged in a process that,

in its way, spelled the downfall of the art of painting, for with the camera and its limitless possibilities came the destruction of the painters' livelihood. I was, indeed, a part of an historical process, and one far more important than Godbolt's murderous but somehow petty scheming.

Stunned by my own thinking, I sat down abruptly.

"What's the matter?"

Lawrence would, I supposed, have understood if I'd been able to articulate what I'd only sensed, but I shook my head. "Nothing. The light's changed."

And then, vainly, I wished for Stefan. Priest. Man. Necessary other.

CHAPTER FIFTEEN

They came up the cañon fast, Godbolt, Fallon, and Sheriff Briscoe in the lead, followed by six others on slower horses.

Lawrence grabbed the bowl and held it against his chest as if fearing another stampede. "Jesus! Can't we get any peace around here?"

I looked around for Jacky, but he'd scurried out of sight. He was probably under his cot in the wagon, and I hoped he was. This boy might have learned from the

Indians, maybe had for all I knew. But he had ears like a cat, and being a fugitive with your life on the line sharpens a person's senses remarkably.

The rest of the crew, obviously remembering Lawrence's warning, had spread out around us, anticipating trouble.

Seeing the set faces of the riders above the tossing heads and manes of their horses, I knew that our peace, such as it was, had ended.

Godbolt dismounted with an agility that belied his age, but his face was that of an old man. "Celine," he said without preamble. "Was she here?"

"Yesterday," I told him. "She came for her photographs, then she left. Has something happened to her?" It was a stupid question. Obviously something had or they wouldn't have been there.

"Her horse came home without her. We've been searching all night." His voice trembled, and for a moment I forgot what I knew he was, saw only the frightened father in the grip of a dread that had driven him to panic.

"Where have you looked?"

"Everywhere. We backtracked her horse, but lost the trail in the rocks. Did she say anything about where she was going? Anything at all?"

"Only that she'd given your man the slip. And that she was going home." As I spoke, I was aware of my own guilt. I'd let that radiant, haughty child ride off alone, knowing she might be in danger. But could I have stopped her? She might have let me ride with her if I'd thought up some plausible excuse. I wondered if that would have saved her, or doomed us both, assuming she had met foul play.

"She said her horse could run faster than anyone else's," I told him, "but I don't think she actually thought it would have to." I must have sounded like a woman making a lame excuse for her own stupidity, because, like all the rest, I assumed that, after she hadn't returned after a whole day, something dreadful must have befallen her.

Godbolt's pale eyes bored into me. "Why do you suppose she said that her horse could outrun anything? Did she act like she suspected she might be in danger?"

"I don't think so. She said that after I told her I was worried about her, Colonel. She was alone and unarmed, and, if I'd thought, I'd have sent someone with her, or gone myself. But she was . . . she was so sure of herself."

"Sounds like her." Fallon spoke from

114

horseback, looking down at us.

Beside me, Lawrence put down the bowl he'd been clutching. "We'll help you look if you'd like. We can cover more country."

Godbolt thought about that a little while, then said: "We can pair you up with my men. You don't know the country. We can make wider sweeps that way."

"I'll go around to the ranches if you think it'll help. Maybe she's hurt and somebody took her in," I offered, needing to do something, anything to help.

"And didn't send a message?" Godbolt looked weary. He knew that some of the settlers would like to cut his daughter's throat to even the score for what he'd done to them.

"It's too early," I said. "We can't assume anything yet."

He nodded once. "You're right, of course," and sounded like he was trying to reassure himself. For a moment he seemed to drift into another world, as if he were listening to voices we couldn't hear. Then he said: "She was all I had. All that was left to me."

The cruel mask that he wore so well had slipped, revealing a man like any other, vulnerable, even helpless in the face of death. For he had, I noticed, used the past tense, as if we were too late, but I think we all thought that, for a reason I can't define.

Moved, I reached out and touched his arm. "We'll do our best," was all I said.

He came suddenly back to the present, influenced perhaps by my genuine sympathy. "All right. You can come with us, Missus Givens, but I want Nash to ride with you to be sure you're safe."

A chill ran up my spine to the top of my head. Godbolt wanted me out of the way and the man he proposed to guard me was his principal *eliminator*. How easy it would be to have another accident and no one to witness it.

I expected Lawrence to protest, but he didn't. All he said at the time was: "Give us a few minutes to saddle up." To me he said: "You don't want to ride one of your work plugs. Take Fan. She's steady as a rock."

I wanted to go with him so we could speak privately, but Godbolt detained me, obviously savoring my dilemma with a grim humor. I saw a suppressed gleam in his eye when he said: "I reckon I know, Missus Givens, how you might have heard bad things about Mister Fallon, but I can assure you they're not true. I brought him here to help the sheriff reëstablish law and order, and, if it'll make you feel better, Nash used to be a Texas Ranger."

At first I thought he was white-washing Fallon for his own purposes, but then realized what he said might be true. Almost every month there were news stories telling how an ex-Ranger had been involved in a shooting, a murder, or a range war.

Fallon looked at me as though seeing me for the first time, his face, as always, unreadable but without any malevolence, then his eyes shifted to Godbolt for a cue as to whether he should say anything. He must have got the nod, though I didn't see it, because he said: "You'll be as safe with me as in church, ma'am, I can assure you."

His Texas drawl was strangely comforting. It put me at my ease for no reason, though my curiosity was piqued about how we'd get along together on our hunt for Celine.

Certainly he was unlike any man I'd ever known. His masculine beauty alone was enough to intrigue not only me but all the women in the valley, even those like May, the woman at the hanging, who, in spite of her hatred, hadn't been able to keep her eyes off him. And then, of course, there'd been Celine. *Had they kissed,* I wondered. *Or had it gone further than that?*

In that brief moment, I wished in vain for Stefan — for his sound advice, his humor, and because he was what he was — a priest and fully conscious of humanity's flaws.

Godbolt was spelling out the directions that each of our pairs of searchers were to take. He looked at Lawrence for confirmation as he said: "We can meet back here at dark."

Lawrence swung up in the saddle. "Suits me. Whoever gets here first can build up a big fire so the rest can see it and come in."

He circled past my wagon, and I saw him bend down, watched his lips move, and knew he was giving Jacky final instructions. Later that night he would tell me he'd told Jacky to go hide in a cave and not come out until he saw two fires burning. He would add with a grin: "I figured if they saw me talking it was because I was cussing my horse."

Over and over people were revealing that they were more than what they seemed. Even Lawrence had suddenly become shrewd and shifty.

We pulled up at the cañon mouth. Although the valley beyond appeared level, it was, in reality, a maze of hidden washes, of hollows hidden by a tapestry of brush, grass, and mesquite — a million places able to conceal a person. The Apaches had known this, had fought the whites using land's own disguise, a shadowy, clever army able to disappear at will. If Celine were anywhere, and hurt, we might ride past within only a few feet away without seeing her. My heart sank.

At first Nash wasn't a talker. Like me, he sat for a minute looking at the country, perhaps deciding where to go or simply thinking his own, private thoughts about the lost girl. Had I misjudged this man just as, in a way, I'd misjudged Godbolt? Had they both, after all, feelings in common with the rest of us?

"Did you see which way she went?" Nash asked me suddenly.

"Straight down the cañon following the trail."

"Did she stick to the trail?"

I tried to recall the small figure on the big horse and shut my eyes, seeing her again in my mind. "It seemed to me she stopped and was looking at something . . . or toward something before she turned off."

"Where?" His voice was urgent.

Again I closed my eyes and visualized what I'd seen. "Maybe about here. I'm not sure."

"Which way was she looking?"

I pointed. "Over there. Toward those hills."

"Come on," he said. "Just stay behind me." He began to walk his horse slowly back and forth, always headed in the direction

119

I'd shown him, always looking intently at the ground.

Watching him, I was fascinated by his concentration, by his grace in the saddle, and then realized what made his features so clearly defined. Undoubtedly he was part Indian.

After a while he moved away on a straight line, never speaking again for over an hour. It was slow, hot travel mostly over rock, and whatever he saw eluded me, though once or twice I spotted what I thought might be a hoof print, half erased by blowing sand.

Finally he pulled up and pointed at an obvious set of tracks. "Her horse," he said. "Every horse has its own track if you know how to read it."

He scanned the surrounding country carefully, probably checking to see if we were being watched, as he had every few minutes even while he had been equally intent on tracking Celine.

We went on this way for hours, he stopping occasionally to let the horses blow, especially after a scramble up some steep terrain. At such times he loosened girths, doing my horse's without being asked, always finding a tree big enough to get us in the shade, and always offering me a drink from his canteen, since in our rush to leave

I'd forgotten to bring one. Then he'd roll and smoke a cigarette before we moved out again. He showed no signs of urgency, and I was grateful for the chance to rest.

The sun rose to its zenith and was working down the western sky when he made our final stop on a hill. At our slow pace, we'd covered perhaps only six or seven miles, though to me it seemed like a hundred. Below us, a small spring bubbled into a rock basin, then overflowed and ran downhill before disappearing into the ground. The horses smelled the water and stamped and tossed their heads, eager to drink.

"Take the horses down and let them drink," Nash said, and something in his voice made me look at him closely, but his face revealed nothing, as usual. "I'm going to go hunt around here on foot. Just don't let them drink too fast at first." The last caution I'm sure he added because he saw me as a kind of greenhorn.

I'm not that much of a greenhorn, I thought, mildly irritated. I knew, as well as he did, that people depended entirely on their horses in this country and sometimes had to think for the horse — even the most seasoned and wise old one.

I was watching the horses blow and cool

their noses in the water, had even bent and splashed some on my own sweaty face, when Nash spoke in my ear.

"Do you want to look at her?"

I had assumed he had been Celine's lover, but, looking at him then, I thought I'd made a wrong assumption. And I don't know what I'd expected of our search, but I hadn't expected him to tell me so calmly and without emotion.

I drew a deep breath to steady myself. I'd seen so many deaths! "I . . . don't . . . I'm not sure."

"You don't have to." He was looking at me with what seemed to be compassion.

"Take my hand," he said, and for the first time his voice trembled.

We skirted the small hill where the spring had its source, and then he parted the brush and I saw what had been beauty transformed as only death can do.

Flies swarmed in her mouth and in her once dancing iris eyes. They crept across her cheeks, buzzed in her nostrils, and in her blood-matted hair. And there was a small hole in her forehead, just such a hole as I'd seen in the gunman who Jacky had shot.

Fighting nausea, I tried without success to remember where Jacky had been the day before — if he'd taken one of our horses and been gone long enough to ambush her. He had the motive, and he had the weapon, and both Nash and I knew it.

Nash stood looking down, his thoughts unfathomable. Killer though he was, he intrigued me, stirred feelings deep in my body that I couldn't control, didn't want to control when he turned and I saw the tears in his eyes.

Without thinking I moved, put my arms around him, felt his physical reaction, as if a spring, deep within, had snapped. No one had ever kissed me the way he did, again and again, his tongue searching my mouth until I thought I'd never forget the taste of him — salt tears and something sweet, like mint. Like a bitch in heat, overcome, seething with emotions too long withheld, I responded. His maleness pressed hard against me, and I knew I couldn't resist his desire.

Then it was over, and not because of anything I did or said. He pushed away suddenly and looked at me with something like shame on his face, and I thought, with some surprise — *Whatever you are now, you were a gentleman once.* — and didn't know whether or not the fact pleased me.

"I'm sorry, but you're a woman," he said,

giving no further explanation for his odd statement.

I have always wondered what would have happened if I'd blurted out the truth. "*I'm not sorry!*" But few women of that day could summon that kind of honesty.

It was, of course, an understandable occurrence. Death's companion is often the passion for life, the lust a denial of our mortality. I know that now. Then I only stared at him, attempting to understand my feelings — and his. Undoubtedly he was a killer. But he was also a man capable of a deep and true love, a man who may have been looking for such a love all his life. Whether or not he'd found it with Celine, I didn't know, but somehow doubted it.

"I'm going to tie her behind my saddle," he said, once again without emotion. "I can't leave her here for the coyotes."

I wondered why the scavengers hadn't found the body before then, and have never found a satisfactory answer. Perhaps a guardian angel was protecting one of God's most perfect creations. I would have liked to think so. The poor child had needed a mother — why not a guardian angel at the end? I was overwhelmed with sadness that she had been taken, and wished that Nash had been with her when she needed him in her last, possibly terrified moments.

We approached camp after dark. All of the others were there, and I could see the colonel by the firelight, seated in one of our camp chairs, staring silently into the flames. He lifted his head at our approach and stood, waiting for our news.

"Is it . . . ?" he asked in a hoarse whisper when Nash began to untie the pathetic bundle.

Nash wasn't one to mince words. "Someone shot her."

I watched the colonel's face crumble as he fought back tears. Then his true nature took over, and he howled his fury like a raging beast.

"Some god-damn' son-of-a-bitch is going to pay for this! I'll burn this whole god-damn' country out! I'll hang every one of those dirty-fingernail bastardly nesters on meat hooks!"

Abruptly he sat down, put his head into his hands, and wept. "My poor beautiful baby! My poor beautiful baby!" he kept saying, a dirge that went on and on while we stood stunned but unable to do more than watch him vent his despair.

I went to bed as soon as I could but was restless all night, missing Jacky asleep in his cot, missing Stefan, wondering where Nash had bedded down and if he was thinking of what had happened between us. Despite my strict Victorian background, and unlike what I had felt with Stefan — though what we'd done was nothing by comparison — I had no feeling of guilt whatsoever about what Nash and I had done.

I was growing up in a way that had never happened even as a married woman. Still I couldn't help but ask myself: *Why him, of all people? A killer.* Then I recalled those surprising tears that had come into his normally cold eyes. I recalled those tears, tasted them on his face, in my mouth as if they were my own.

I had comforted him at the time of his great need. *Nothing more will come of it!* I assured myself, but I wasn't reassured and dreamed of our passion again, with the same incomplete ending. I was reaching out for what was not there, for a ghost that vanished before it could be touched.

CHAPTER SIXTEEN

In the morning I was cranky and tired, thankful when all of Godbolt's party left with Celine's body carefully stowed in one of our wagons. I didn't see Nash anywhere among those who loaded her, and wondered where he was.

I made breakfast, and we all ate in silence, painfully aware that Jacky hadn't come back. Finally Lawrence couldn't hold in his thoughts any longer.

He took the floor like an oracle, pronouncing as only he could. "We all know that Celine was killed by a Twenty-Two bullet. And we all know that our young friend killed one of Godbolt's men the same way. What we have to decide is what we're going to do now. We're vulnerable and will be if it's discovered we're harboring a murderer."

"Jacky couldn't have done it! You all must know that!" I jumped up, bumping the table and spilling my coffee, forced into defending Jacky even though I, too, had some doubts.

"Then why's he still hiding?" Lawrence wanted to know.

"He's scared out of his wits and smart!" I snapped. "He didn't see two fires last night like you said you'd build if the coast was clear, so he knows we let them stay in camp. He probably still isn't sure we won't sell him out, especially for money, and he knows Godbolt has that. Besides, it's early yet. He might be sneaking down here right now, being careful that nobody's going to nab him."

Hugh was mopping up the spill. "Suppose

they already have nabbed him? Godbolt's probably had someone watching our camp. Anyone half smart would, and he's no dummy."

I could read on Lawrence's face that he hadn't thought of that and didn't like the notion at all. He liked his privacy, and his work space, and he liked Jacky in spite of the gruff exterior he showed the kid most of the time. I thought his ranting now was more like whistling in the dark than his true feeling — hoping someone would reassure him just as I had done.

"Yes. Well. . . . That's just what we need. Spies up on the cliffs. Are we ever going to be allowed to get some work done?"

"I think you should do just that," I said. "Everybody act normal . . . or try to. What else can we do?"

He looked relieved at my simple solution. "Good idea. You boys get back to work. I have some papers I need to look at and I want a moment with you, Sidra."

I'd known he had something more on his mind than Jacky and was dying to unburden himself. "Be with you after I clean up," I said.

"Leave it!" He watched the crew disperse, then turned to me. "You aren't going to believe this," he started.

128

"Try me," I said.

"Let's go over and sit under my tent awning and get out of the sun. This is going to take a while."

When we were settled in camp chairs, he started in with a huge sigh. "When I went out with Trig yesterday we wandered all over the country and stopped at several ranches. We got quite a reception, especially from a family named Arnason. Trig knows all those folks and isn't afraid to ride right up to their doors. I'd think twice about it after the receptions we got, but he's either got a lot of guts, or very little brains.

Most likely both, I thought.

"When we got to Arnasons the old man came out on his porch, packing a double barrel scatter-gun. His woman was right behind him with her hands folded in front of her like at church, and her apron balled up around them. I figured she had a six-shooter under the apron.

"Anyhow, when Trig told them what we were there for, the old man yelled loud enough to scare the sparrows out of the trees. 'Just turn around and ride out the way you come in! There's no gal here.' But he was scared. Damn scared. I wondered if he knew more than he wanted to let on.

"The old biddy wasn't too scared to give

129

me the once-over. She asked me who I was, and, when I told her, she said they knew I'd thrown in with Godbolt and so had my woman."

He leered at me, or tried to. Lawrence really isn't the leering type. "How does it feel to be 'my woman'?"

I didn't rise to the bait, simply gave him a look, and he went on.

"I told her Celine was missing, maybe hurt, and that it wasn't her fault what was happening, but all I got from the old girl was . . . 'Like father, like daughter. Maybe this'll teach him a lesson.'

"Old Arnason was waving the shotgun around so much I was worried he might accidentally shoot us. He didn't like May mouthing at us, either. He started cussing her and us, yelled at her to get in the house."

"May?" I interrupted. "You're sure that's her name?"

"That's what he called her."

"She's the woman who was at the hanging. They're both scared out of their wits . . . you're right about that. But they're not going to run out, either."

"Can't blame them," he said. "Without Godbolt, this place is close to paradise." Then he went on. "May didn't go right back in, probably because the old man ordered her to, just stood there looking sour as hell. I told her the girl was still a child, and if they saw anything, to let us know. And I said not to judge us by the company we kept. It didn't change her attitude one bit. Old May is a first-class sneerer.

"She gave me a sermon on how somebody should've spanked sense into Celine, taken her over their knee . . . you know the kind of talk. Then she said we might as well 'git', that they were taking care of themselves because the Lord had turned his back on honest folks. You get the idea?"

I did, indeed, having observed their behavior at close range. "Then what?" I asked.

"Then we got. I looked back once, just to make sure the old man wasn't having second thoughts about shooting us out of the saddle, and there they were, the two of them side-by-side, looking like God's wrath. Quite a picture."

I could see them in my mind's eye, solid as rocks and unyielding. When the trouble was over — if it ever was — I hoped I could photograph some of these people — not the wealthy ranchers like Godbolt, but those who were the backbone of the frontier.

So far there was nothing very startling about Lawrence's story — only the picture of the old couple that lingered in my head, but I listened as he went on.

"We visited two more places . . . the Kellogg and Buhl homesteads, according to Trig . . . and got the same kind of reception. By then it was late afternoon, and we were both hot and sweaty, and I was getting damn' tired of looking down the barrels of shotguns. It seems like everybody in the valley owns at least two. Then Trig said he knew from the start nobody would tell us anything, even if they knew. They were more apt to hope Godbolt's fancy daughter was down a mine shaft or maybe in a cave somewhere."

"Then why'd he bother?" I asked. I was becoming irritated with the way Lawrence was dragging out what he could have told me in a couple sentences.

He dug in his shirt pocket for his tobacco pouch and put it on the table. "I asked him that. I asked why he hung around in a place like this one, and he said something that surprised me. He'd been in Lincoln County during the trouble years ago, and got out of there, but now he's got a family to support and is saving up to go to Colorado and try to raise chickens and a garden. He says his wife grew up on a farm, and she's ready to leave when he gives the word. She's as sick of it all as everybody else, it seems."

"I wonder how many other of Godbolt's men are ready to jump ship," I said. "Probably a lot more than we think. But when do we get to the unbelievable part? So far all this makes perfect sense."

He laughed. "A good story has to drag out a little. How about making us some more coffee and laying out a slice of that apple pie if the boys haven't raided it?"

I did that, and he polished off his pie in short order, got his pipe going to suit him, leaned back in his chair, and said: "Now where was I?"

"You just left two shotgun-totin' homesteaders named Kellogg and Whatsis, and Trig's telling you he wants out."

"Now it gets interesting." Rather than continue, he puffed on his pipe and watched the smoke rise.

"I'm waiting with baited breath," I said, hoping to stir him out of his complacency.

"Well, we rode down into the river bottom, and smelled smoke. Trig said he'd go ahead and check it out, and I went right along with him. We found a wagon tucked away beside the river . . . and a boy about Jacky's age carrying the same kind of little slide action Winchester Twenty-Two, only his had seen a lot more hard wear. He had his sister with him, and they looked like a

133

pair of ragamuffins. I thought we'd found another set of orphans, but Trig knew them and asked where their mother was.

"The boy looked scared, but held onto that rifle like he knew how to use it and wasn't afraid to. Probably just as capable as Jacky. But all he said about his mother was . . . 'She's out.'

"Trig didn't care for that answer. Neither did I, come to think of it. Trig is a deputy, after all. So he asked the kid what they were doing there."

Lawrence smiled, remembering the next part. "The kid gave us a nasty look and said . . . 'There ain't no law ag'in' it.' Then Trig bawled him out, until he admitted his mother was hunting dinner. The whole time the little girl just stood there, watching. Pretty as a penny, but nobody'd combed her hair for a week. You'd have probably decided to adopt them both."

"I might," I said. "You can never tell."

"Along with Jacky? Even now?" He wasn't one to let go an idea easily.

"Especially now," I said. "He needs me. And maybe I'll even adopt you and the crew and charge board."

At that he laughed out loud. "I almost believe you."

"You'd better."

And Nash, I thought. *I'd like to adopt Nash, too.* Certainly he didn't need a mother, but he needed something, and had seen it in me. And I'd needed something, too, and wasn't about to dodge the knowledge. *Oh, Stefan, what have you started?* I said silently, for whatever was happening to me had its roots in that moment when he'd reached out and held me.

Lawrence would have had apoplexy if he'd read my mind, but he was more interested in his story. "We tried to tell the kids what we were there about, but the boy wouldn't listen, and we left. On the way back, Trig told me their mother's Harve's widow. And homeless as a result."

I sat up in my chair. "We've got to help them. I can take some food down. Maybe they'll talk to me . . . or she will. And you said the boy had a Twenty-Two?"

He nodded. "And knew what it was for, if I'm any judge. As for taking food . . . well, you'd better take that Forty-One of yours along. The way Trig tells it, the woman has lost her mind. He told me something else, too. A real shocker."

I knew I was in for a long session, so I settled back in my chair, and let Lawrence go into his oracular mode.

"After we rode out of there, Trig stopped

135

to roll a cigarette. He looked like he had something on his chest he wanted to get off, and that's an understatement if there ever was one. He eyed me for a while as though he was trying to decide whether to trust me or not. Maybe with the load he was carrying, he didn't care whether or not he could trust me.

"Finally he just started in, and it was like a dam had burst. He said that after he saw that dead girl and the kid the other day, he told his wife all about it. She's a Mexican, and the way he put it . . . 'Mexicans is as close-mouthed as Injuns when they want to be,' . . . so he wasn't really taking any chances. He showed her a gold medallion he'd taken off the body, and she asked if she could show it around to see if anybody knew whose it was. She waited until the next day to tell Trig what she found out. Was scared even to tell him, because he works for the sheriff, which means he works for Godbolt. Anyhow, according to her, the whole Mexican community knew who the medal belonged to."

Lawrence stopped and went through the motions of getting his pipe lit again, much to my exasperation.

"For God's sake, don't stop now! Who was she?" I pounded on the arm of my chair.

He chuckled, then dropped his thunder-bolt. "The colonel's mistress. Her name was María Gonzalez. The kid was his."

My mouth dropped open in surprise. Then common sense won out. Of course, a man like Godbolt would have a mistress — even bastard children. But mistresses, especially Mexican women, didn't just wander off away from their protectors, at least not without a good reason.

"How come Godbolt hasn't missed them?" I asked. "I mean . . . it's been about a month, maybe more. You'd think he'd wonder where she was."

"Good question. And this is where the whole thing gets 'curiouser and curiouser', as Alice would put it. Godbolt thinks they're at his ranch down in Mexico. Trig told me Godbolt wanted them out of the way before he started the real trouble. That kid was the apple of his eye, and I'd guess he must've loved the woman. What I can't figure is why he didn't get Celine out, too, but maybe he got over-confident. Thought he could pro-tect her until at least after her party."

"And got her murdered," I said. "So who did kill the mistress? Did Trig have any ideas?"

Lawrence puffed away and watched the smoke disappear. Then he said: "Just hear me out and see if you agree with me. Trig told me then that Godbolt had Celine, Fallon, old Juan, and Roberto, another of his *pistoleros,* take María out at night to the railroad at Sacaton. Celine was supposed to go to Mexico with María and the kid, then come home. And Roberto, like every other man in the valley, was trying to make time with Celine, but didn't have a chance with Fallon along. Being the kind of man he is, he could have shot Celine himself, in one of those Latin fits of jealousy, come to think of it, but that's doubtful.

"Anyhow, he came back with Fallon and Juan, and a week later Celine came back, so she may have actually seen María safe at the ranch in Mexico. Why shouldn't she since anything else would have raised some pretty grave suspicions in Godbolt if he found out . . . and he sure would have in time. If she did, that'll come out, and we'll have the big mystery then of why María came back, since she and the kid ended up here in the cave. I'm having a hard time trying to figure if Celine was hard enough to have looked so innocent at her party, knowing that María and the kid were dead, if she did. As far as that goes, we're assuming a lot in thinking she had the girl killed. Suppose old Godbolt was tired of María and put on a good face so the Mexican community was fooled by it?"

"Wait a minute," I said. "This is getting a little too thick. This can't all be happening under Godbolt's nose, with him not knowing about it. Seems to me like he knows everything that's going on."

Lawrence looked wise. "Maybe he does and maybe he doesn't. If he had the job done, then he does. But if he didn't, who would tell him? It's a cinch nobody wants to talk about it because the guilt might just fall on them.

"The way I see it, Celine probably had Fallon kill María and cart her body up here, so those two aren't going to say anything. I wouldn't put it past Celine to have been pulling the strings on Fallon right under her daddy's nose for a long time."

The way *I* saw it, nobody played puppetmaster with Nash, but this wasn't the time to say so. I did, though, have to give Lawrence higher marks for observation than I'd ever given him before. Apparently he'd penetrated to the granite behind Celine's innocent eyes.

I said: "But this is supposition, based on Celine being the guilty one. What reason would she have to kill María . . . or the boy? I mean . . . she seemed so innocent. And she was so beautiful."

" 'Beauty is as beauty does', to quote an old saying. And there's more to it." Lawrence tapped the ash out of his pipe. "From what Trig said, Celine hated María because of the kid. It would have been easy for her to kill them both somewhere along the way. It was her behind it all right, whether she killed them personally or not."

I remembered the look in her eyes the night of the party, and how she'd seemed to be hiding a secret. Like her father, she was no fool. "She was too smart to be within ten miles of the killing, if you ask me. But let's say she did it. Why did the bodies end up at the cave? Her idea? Or convenience? Why here of all places? And was she strong enough to lug them all the way up there?"

"Fallon," Lawrence said succinctly. "They could have been killed anywhere. Even in Mexico and carted up here. Hell, they could have put the bodies on a train. Money talks in Mexico. As a matter of fact, it talks everywhere if you have enough of it. Anyhow, after the bodies got in this neck of the woods, Fallon could've put them in the dead wagon. Everybody around is used to the sight of it, and they don't dare go to check on who's in it. Maybe the caves are where they dump the bodies. Fallon would know that . . . and he'd have figured it's as safe a place as any."

Anything was possible in such a violent country, of course. I recalled the disappearance of Judge Fountain and his son a few years before. Who knew where their bodies were? Everyone figured they were buried in some isolated place. But regardless of what I'd been told about Nash poisoning Granny Prosser, I couldn't believe he was capable of killing a woman, much less an infant, and in the vastness of the Lost River Valley there were a thousand easier places to hide bodies.

I said as much to Lawrence, who looked pleased at my powers of deduction. "Questions, questions," he said. "Maybe we've stumbled onto where the dead wagon really does dump the bodies. Think about that. Then think about why Godbolt's men tried to run us out of here, despite the old boy swearing that wasn't so. Some of those caves go quite a ways back into the mountain."

"I guess when the coroner comes up here, maybe we'd better organize a little search party," I said.

Lawrence laughed. "Do you really think bodies might be in the caves? I was shooting the moon there to see how you'd take it."

"Why not? It all makes a crazy sort of sense. Especially when I was listening to you tell it."

Lawrence said: "While we're shooting the moon, let's allow that maybe Godbolt isn't the only madman in the valley. We may be barking up the wrong tree entirely. Maybe somewhere there's another nutty one . . . possibly several, with their own stack of corpses in the making."

"Stop it!" I implored. My head was spinning. I have always found it difficult to take in too much information at one time, but once again I went back to what was bothering me.

"Well, about the one body we're sure of, sooner or later Godbolt's going to find out. If he really did love María and the boy, then all hell's going to break loose. And someone has to tell him. The cat is on the sheriff's back now. Trig has to tell him or leave the country."

Lawrence snorted. "It won't be any of the Mexicans that tell him, that's for sure. For example, can you imagine a nice little, inoffensive old man, a servant like Juan for instance, telling Godbolt? He'd quake in his boots at the thought he'd be blamed. Don't forget the custom of killing the messenger who brings bad tidings."

"We're going 'round and 'round," I said wearily. "Let's stop running in circles. From what you say, you really believe it was Celine who killed María."

"Or Fallon, with Celine behind him." He said it emphatically. "Fallon would have gone along because he hoped to marry Celine and inherit the old man's fortune."

"No!" I spoke louder than I'd intended, and he stared at me for a minute.

"Why not?"

For the first time in my life I felt myself blushing and hoped he didn't notice. "Because . . . he didn't act like he'd been her. . . ." I hesitated, unable to say the word.

"Lover." Lawrence supplied it. "Of course, he was. It was plain as the nose on your face. Which, by the way, is red as a beet. Better get out of the sun."

I stood up, grateful that he hadn't guessed the reason why I had rushed to Nash's defense and changed the subject.

"If you can spare me and tell me where Mercy and her kids are, I'll take them something to eat."

"I'll go with you. It's best not to wander around here by yourself. And I'd carry that Forty-One with you wherever you go from now on. There's no telling what's going to happen. The boys will have to make out the

143

best way they know how. So will Jacky, if he comes back."

His last words struck me to the heart. How could one small boy, even one capable of shooting a man, manage to survive with what seemed like luck always against him?

I said a small prayer for the little ragamuffin I'd come to love, and wished it on its way toward God with all my might.

CHAPTER SEVENTEEN

I put together as much food as I thought we could spare — or as much as I thought Lawrence would let me give away. There were times when he, out of some inherited Puritan notion, became a penny-pincher. I was prepared to argue that I could go to town for more anytime, but thought of all the arguments that would invite from the good Dr. Haslett, especially in view of Celine's disappearance and murder. I was sure our next shopping trip would look like a cavalry troop if he had anything to say about it.

Lawrence jumped in to drive the wagon without even checking what I had put into it. We headed down the river on our mission of mercy, and I breathed a heavy sigh of relief. He could be a cross to bear at times, but this wasn't going to be one of them.

"Hello, the camp!" I called when, from a small rise, I could look into the clearing where the wagon listed to one side on a damaged wheel.

No one answered. Around us the silence was complete as if I'd suddenly gone deaf. Even the cottonwoods that usually danced were still.

Lawrence tied the team to a small willow bush, and we went forward on foot.

Fear is a strange emotion, and it was fear of what we might find that forced me forward into the clearing, but, except for the wagon and the ashes of an old fire, the place could have been abandoned a year before.

A wisp of smoke from those ashes alerted me. Someone, not long before, had been here, was probably even now hiding in the brush watching us. Waiting.

I took a breath, then swallowed my fear. "Mercy Fellows!" I called. "If you're here, come out. We're friends." Then I waited in the silence broken now only by the *buzz* of a locust.

"I got no friends, and what d'you want?" Mercy materialized like a ghost, the shotgun sweeping over both of us.

"I brought you some food."

"Git yer damned poison eats out of here, and you with 'em." Her eyes, when I forced myself to look into them, were as blank as Fallon's. Killer eyes.

But I have always hated giving up. "Your children are hungry. Please, won't you take it for them?"

She came toward me. "I know about your tricks. I've seen 'em before, and it wasn't pretty watchin' poor old Granny Prosser die, a-holdin' her hand, waitin' fer a doctor that never got there. Now git!"

That was too much for Lawrence. He exploded: "You think we'd poison you? You're mad! Put down that damned shotgun. We aren't here to hurt anybody."

"You wuz with that toad, Trig, yesterday," she snapped. "I don't even know who you are."

In his most pompous, academic voice, Lawrence said: "I am Doctor Lawrence Haslett, representing the Smithsonian Institution in Washington, D.C."

She probably had no idea what the Smithsonian Institution was and, if she did, wouldn't have cared. But the words "Doctor" and "Washington D.C." hit home. It was an age when learned doctors and professors and ministers impressed Ameri-

146

can matrons, even on the frontier. If Dr. So-and-So said it, then it must be true.

The gun didn't waver, but she cocked her head. "I'm listenin'. But you better talk fast and make sense."

Lawrence said: "I'm an archeologist and I came here to study the old Indian ruins. I had no idea what I was getting into. Sidra Givens here is our photographer and a famous one." I realized he was stretching it for effect. "She didn't know what she was getting into, either. She saw your husband hang, and then had to help Jacky Chastain get his father's body in a wagon and carry it away before the dead wagon came. I don't blame you for thinking somebody you saw with Trig might poison you, but I was only helping look for a lost girl."

That turned her on again. "That one. Serves her right if she's dead. An' her old man, too. He can find out how we feel when his hired guns kill our folks. We may be poor, but we can hurt just as much as anyone when somebody we love dies!"

Though I remembered that I'd thought she was beyond tears, I could see the glint of them in her eyes. "The girl is dead. We found her body yesterday." I said it as much to bring her out of her sorrow as anything else. This wasn't really the time to tell her.

In fact, she had no business knowing.

It occurred to me that she had a .22 — or her boy did — and she wasn't that far from where Nash and I had found Celine. Revenge is as good a motive as any, and Mercy was certainly capable of killing in a fit of madness.

If I saw Nash again alone, I'd ask him if he'd seen the killer's tracks. For all I knew, he'd gone back to the spot and was following those tracks right now. And if they led him here, he could be watching us. I glanced around, just in case.

Mercy noticed. "If yer lookin' for the kids, I told 'em to hide and not come out when we heard you comin' through the brush like a circus parade." Slowly she lowered the shotgun. "I'll take your truck, and I'm sorry if I misjudged you, but who could blame me? I've lost everything but my kids and I aim to keep them alive. But it'll take more'n eats to do that if I'm any judge."

"It's a start."

"Yer right there. I can feel my belly button a-ticklin' my backbone right now." She cackled over that and maybe over the prospect of doing something about it. "Leave yer truck and go on back where you come from. We'll make out fine without you."

"For how long?"

148

Without the protection of the shotgun, she looked like what she was — a woman who'd lost everything and was struggling against the odds.

"Long as it takes me to get rid of those bastards. I have plans."

"Mercy . . . ," I began.

She cut me off. "That's a good one. I got no Mercy left. Not now. Nobody showed me or Harve any, or that poor old woman, neither, and I never did believe in turnin' the other cheek. I believe that God helps those that help theirselves, and I'm doin' my part, and not you nor anybody's goin' to stop me. I'll dance on their graves and a lot of folks here'll dance with me."

As she rambled on, her expression changed until she became again the mad woman I'd seen at the hanging — a woman capable of revenge — and of murder. I doubted anything I said would reach her, but I tried, using the only weapon I had.

"You just admitted you have children to protect. Think of them."

She cackled again. "My kids are smart, and I'm teachin' 'em what they need to get along. Somebody has to. Now I've listened enough, talked enough. Do what I told you and git!" But she made no motion to take up her shotgun again.

We left enough food to tide her over a few days. I looked back and waved, but she didn't see me. She was already starting to build up a cooking fire before we were out of sight. The kids had come out of hiding and were inspecting the bags of food.

Lawrence shot me a look. "Did you notice anything strange back there?"

"It was all pretty strange, but no," I said. "I was too busy watching that crazy old woman and her shotgun. What?"

"There must have been the tracks of a dozen shod horses around. Maybe we just found out who runs that nester army that shot up Godbolt's place."

It was a new thought. And I was impressed with how wilderness wise the good doctor was getting.

"Splendid deduction, Sherlock." I couldn't resist teasing him a little.

And he couldn't resist a smart retort. "Thank you very much, Doctor Watson."

Another thought brought me back to sobriety. Suppose Nash was following the tracks of Celine's killer and they led him to Mercy? And suppose she had a gang hidden out in the brush?

I looked back over my shoulder, half expecting to hear gunfire. What I heard was silence — the silence of the river bottom.

Wind, leaves in motion, the calling of birds. Then I laughed at myself. Nash was no fool, certainly not fool enough to blunder into an ambush. But was he really, as Lawrence and a lot of others were all too ready to believe, a woman and baby killer?

CHAPTER EIGHTEEN

The next day was the day of Celine's funeral. And Jacky still hadn't returned. Surely, I thought, he'd have come in or gotten word to us. Surely, unless — I couldn't bring myself to formulate it in words, but thought: *He may never have a funeral. He could be dead somewhere with a fly-blown body like Celine's. Dead and waiting for that awful wagon to carry him off.* With a heavy heart I climbed onto our own wagon seat beside Lawrence.

The road to the ranch was once again clogged with traffic — mourners and those who came simply out of curiosity — but this time there was no music or laughter, only the creaking of wagons and saddle leather, the rhythmic drumbeat of hoofs on hard ground.

Lawrence and I argued back and forth over whether, when, and *especially if* we should tell Godbolt about María. Lawrence stated the principal argument against it.

"If we think what will happen to this country over his losing Celine is terrible, I can only imagine what will happen if he learns he's lost the only two other people he loved."

"He'll find out sooner or later."

"Better later. And better from somebody else. I'm thinking of pulling out until all this blows over."

Leave! He wanted to leave? I turned on him, shocked. "You'd desert all these helpless people?"

"They're not our problem."

"Maybe not yours. But I'm not sorry to say that I can't share your detachment." When he didn't answer, I added: "I'm not leaving Jacky here alone." And I wasn't leaving until Stefan came back.

"What makes you think we'll ever see Jacky again?"

Lawrence could be cruelly blunt, but showed no sign that he realized he had. It was a thought I couldn't bring myself to face. But it was a possibility. In my heart Jacky was already my son, and I couldn't, wouldn't, leave him. The thought of never seeing Stefan again left me even more bereft, as if I'd lost the one person who saw me as I was. What had happened between

Nash and me was momentary, the blind seeking of one animal for another. What I felt for Stefan seemed a gift, though an unlikely one.

"Let's just stop talking about it," I said. "We can't very well go to the funeral and hit Godbolt over the head with two more bodies, one of them his son's. It's not right, even though he deserves it."

Lawrence pulled back on the reins and brought the team to a stop in front of the *hacienda*. "If the opportunity comes up, we're morally bound to do it to save everybody trouble in the long run. But Trig's life won't be worth a nickel if Godbolt learns he held out. We could mention seeing a peculiar medallion on the body, and let him take it from there."

"And hope that Trig's smart enough to play dumb." A solution that I couldn't believe.

"For all we know, he may have already told Briscoe to clear his skirts, and maybe the sheriff has already told Godbolt. In any case, we may be about to find out."

A gray-faced Godbolt stood in the *zaguán* — a man far removed from the assured, proud *jefe* I'd first met. He seemed in a daze, accepting condolences as if someone else stood in his boots and spoke the ritual words for him.

We paid our respects and moved on, since there were others who crowded up to do the same thing. I doubt that Godbolt even recognized many of them, am not sure he recognized us, but at least my condolences were sincere and not offered merely to stay in his good graces. On that day I truly pitied him and deplored Celine's death, killer or not, and I still wasn't entirely convinced of her guilt.

Once we'd moved out of hearing, Lawrence said: "I have some circulating to do. Briscoe's here. Maybe we can find out if Trig tipped him off." He drifted away.

Celine lay in the large room to the right of the door, her hands crossed at her breast. It seemed that she was only sleeping there, a fairy princess waiting for a kiss to waken her. Godbolt had brought in a professional embalmer from Albuquerque, and he'd done a magnificent job. Even the wound in her head was carefully masked by art.

I stood a long time, looking down, erratic thoughts chasing through my head. There was Edward in his grave far to the north, Chastain and his wife, the colonel's mistress and child, all of them gone, swiftly and with finality. Somewhere there was a thread binding all together; a single strand that made

154

sense out of a scrambled tapestry, and I had hold of one end of it. There were still questions to be cleared up, but that would not be done by the local authorities. I hoped almost against hope that the U.S. would step into the case and send an investigator as they had in Lincoln and Colfax Counties in earlier days, when violence had torn them apart. The wars came to a halt during its presence, each side fearing to offend and tip the justice department's decision against them.

I said my farewell to Celine. Whatever her faults, she had been a presence, and, when the colonel discovered that he'd also lost María and his child, he would be facing the future with nothing to love. All that was left him would be revenge.

And then there was Nash. What had Celine really meant to him? Probably at most passion, and a ticket to a lifetime of wealth. Nash, though, didn't impress me as power mad, or very much interested in any kind of power except what he had the guts to fight for. Like all of his kind, he was a proud one, a lion sure of its supremacy, ready to fight all challengers.

I sensed someone standing behind me and turned to find Nash watching me. As usual, his face betrayed nothing.

Without stopping to think, I asked: "Did you go back to track the killer?"

For once he looked surprised and took his time answering. When he did, he was blunt. "Yes."

"And?" I wasn't going to let him off that easily.

"The only tracks I found besides Celine's horse led back here to the ranch." The tone of his voice was without innuendo, but I knew he could recognize the tracks of most of the ranch horses.

"That doesn't make sense," I said, wondering if the killer had borrowed a horse from the ranch remuda.

He shrugged. "Maybe it does."

What did he know? Perhaps whoever killed Celine had had a right to do it in his eyes. On the other hand, it was possible that he'd already taken care of the killer but chose to remain silent. The dead wagon served many useful purposes.

I gave up trying to find answers in his face, and thought it was a good time to stop prying for fear of getting in too deep. Instead, I looked at Celine. "She's as beautiful as I remember her."

"I knew her better than anyone. Better even than her daddy," he said.

"Did you love her?" I realized I was

overstepping good manners, and quickly added: "I'm sorry. That's none of my business."

He smiled for the first time I could recall, his eyes warming a little. "She would have been hard to love. And she was just a kid, really."

I wondered if his words "would have been" were carefully chosen. Nash was by no means merely the gun-slinging cowboy many took him to be. In any case I'd found out what I wanted to know. He hadn't loved her. Probably hadn't done more than kiss her. I wasn't deceiving myself about why that answer was important to me. I felt the pull of the man even here in the sacred presence of death. Perhaps especially here.

He changed the subject and gave me his arm. "Let me get you something to eat."

I accepted his escort to the dining room where the tables were loaded with what amounted to a banquet. Even in his grief, Godbolt hadn't forgotten his duties as host. He knew there would be mourners who had risen before daybreak, traveled a long way as we had, and would be hungry. I looked at the table, thinking I really couldn't eat much, then turned and saw Nash leaving the room. I wondered why he'd told me as much as he had. And why I cared.

Of course, I knew the answer to that. Passion, however brief, wipes out differences. It no longer mattered that he was a killer. What mattered was what we had shared, the knowledge that it could happen again, that our hunger lay just below the surface — controlled, masked, but vital.

Hugh Stiles and Dan de Vries approached from the opposite side of the dining room, delighted by the sight of the bounty — a meal quite different from my plain camp cooking.

Dan was beaming over a heaped plate. "This guy doesn't stint, does he?" He gestured at the table with a massive silver fork. "Looks like a banquet for the President."

"It's all he's got left," I said. "Fine china, expensive silver, and land."

"It'd be enough for me. But it's too bad about the girl. She was something. Who'd have believed this would happen the other day when she was with us and so full of fun?"

Fun? I wondered. *Maybe. And maybe also "murder most foul".*

"Somebody out there is a murderer," I said to prevent him from being carried away.

"Could be right here in this room." He looked around with what seemed like excitement at the very thought.

"Hush!" I said, hoping we hadn't been overheard. All I saw were people occupied with food, and a pair of red-eyed servant girls who looked like they'd been weeping for days.

One of them came to stand beside me when Dan and Hugh moved away. "The *señora* doesn't eat." It was both statement and question.

To please her, I picked up a plate. "I'm not very hungry."

She nodded. "A sad time."

"And now?"

The girl stared at her feet in rope sandals, then muttered: "She was his heart, *señora*. Now . . . who can say?"

As if she had said too much, she moved away, shoulders hunched. A sudden notion took me to get more out of her.

"Wait." I put out a hand to stop her. "Do you mean Celine, or María? Didn't she and the boy have his heart, too?"

She looked both startled and frightened, as if she thought I might be a *bruja* with second sight. "You know about that?"

When I nodded in the affirmative, she clasped her hands together, wondering, I suppose, if she could trust me. Then she motioned me to one side.

Out of hearing of any others, she said: "Did you think we were weeping for the blonde one? It was María and the boy we loved. The colonel loved his son, *señora*. Many times we would watch him take the child up onto his saddle, and he would tell us how his son would someday make a fine *charro*. Then he would make the horse trot around the corral, and they would laugh together, and we would all clap our hands and make the horse go faster. María, she tell us that the *señor* promised her he would take care of her and the boy even after he was dead. But now María is gone, and the boy is gone, may God bless them, and it is the *señor* who has nothing and no one to care. He wonders why she is not here in time for the funeral."

So Trig had told the truth when he said that Godbolt had loved María and the boy. If that were not true, Godbolt himself might have eliminated a mistress gone stale, but this story ruled that out, and I was glad of it. Still, there was a murderer out there — or perhaps two — waiting to strike for different motives. "No one has told him yet that María is dead?" I asked.

"We are all afraid, *señora*. Of what he will do."

"Someone murdered her. We found her

160

body in the cave."

"They told us, but not that you knew who she was. They told us how María and the boy looked with their souls gone to *Dios*." Her hand trembled as she made the sign of the cross. "Who would do this terrible thing?"

"I don't know any more than you," I said. "I thought maybe you could tell me."

"I only work in the kitchen, *señora*. What goes on in other places, I don't know."

But I thought she did know. "How is Juan?" I asked before she could escape. She again looked at me in fright, as though now she was sure I was a witch.

"You know about him?"

I nodded sagely, sure that the less I said the more she would say, but she remained silent, fearful, and obviously wishing to leave, so I said: "I know Celine ran away without him the day she was killed, and then she laughed about it."

"It was a game, *señora*. Always she played it. She was young and wild and life did not move fast enough for her. But what could Juan do? She cared for no one but herself, but he had to take care of her because of her father."

Was she saying that Juan hadn't liked Celine? Well, that wasn't impossible. It seemed no one had really loved her except the colonel — and someone had hated her enough to murder her.

"You mean the colonel could have fired him?" I asked.

"No. Because the *señor* loved María."

This made no sense, and the girl seemed to recognize that she had simply confused me. "You knew Juan was María's father?" she said in a whisper.

I felt like I'd been stabbed between the shoulder blades. Here was a new suspect for the killing of Celine, one with a real motive if he had somehow discovered that Celine had killed his daughter.

The girl must have divined from my astonishment that I hadn't known that Juan was María's father and was smart enough to know what her loose mouth had just done to Juan.

I wondered what the colonel would do when he discovered that Celine might have killed his mistress and son. And what would he do if he learned that Juan also knew the truth? In Godbolt's twisted mind, Juan would immediately become the prime suspect, his own life in danger.

This girl was no fool. She had figured that out, too. They probably all thought Juan had done it, maybe knew that he had.

"Please, *señora,* tell no one what I have told you," she said, fear in her eyes. "I want no trouble, and Juan . . . he is not himself." She held tightly to my hand and implored me with her dark eyes. She said: "I can tell that you are a good and kind woman. Please don't get us in any more trouble. Juan has already died in his heart. He loved her, too. And the boy. Now he has no one."

With that, she slipped away quickly on sandaled feet, and left me thinking of the danger all around. I now knew too much, and life was held cheaply here. And it all was because of the ambitions of the man who stood, grieving and humbled in the *zaguán,* a man who had made his threats and had already shown he was capable of carrying them out.

Everything that happened in the valley could be seen as a series of moves, right or wrong, a game we could not help but lose in the end, and yet we played it, all of us, every minute of our days.

It was a slow, sad procession that made its way to the graveyard on its small rise behind the house. We walked, following the wagon that carried Celine — a long line of mourners, many of whom, quite possibly, were not what they seemed.

The cemetery was walled off from the surrounding brush, but inside all was taken care of well. An ornate headstone guarded what was only a monument to Celine's mother, since she'd died long ago in Mexico, unless Godbolt had had her remains moved here. It would be like him. And beside that cenotaph was the naked hole in the red earth where her daughter would rest. Flowers were massed at the graveside, an incongruous blaze of color valiantly resisting the mood of this forlorn place in the high desert.

The minister droned on, and to forget him and his empty ritual I searched the faces of those who stood, hands folded, eyes cast down. Was there a killer here gloating over seeing his victim to her final reward, or was he or she somewhere else, watching and waiting for a chance at the colonel — or Nash?

As always, Nash's expression was blank, although a muscle in his cheek twitched as if he was making an effort at control. The sheriff, I noticed, kept nervously tugging at his drooping mustache. I conjectured that he wanted to be gone, far away from possible trouble. In the gathering of neighbors, cowboys, gunmen, and servants, I saw the Mexican girl who had spoken to me, her fingers moving over the beads of her rosary, her lips moving as she prayed. She may not have loved Celine, but she had been raised to respect the dead, and to keep her true feelings hidden for fear of retribution. Beside her, stood a man, old in years but with that ageless face so common in this country, hewn out of rock and burned brown by years of sun and wind.

Like me, he was alert, his glittering black eyes moving from one person to the next. He stared at me for a long moment in which I forced myself not to look away from what was both assessment and judgment. I knew this had to be Juan, and I wondered if the girl had confessed to him that she had told me too much. When, with a slight nod, he dismissed me, I let out the breath I'd been holding. Whether or not he was Celine's killer, there was a basic honesty, a strength about him that I responded to.

He would have been a stand-out in any group, and Lawrence, noticing him, bent over and whispered in my ear. "Who do you suppose that dignified old Mexican is?"

"Not here!" I hoped he wouldn't press the point and he didn't.

The prayers, the eulogy, seemed endless. For the first time I was glad that Edward had had only Lawrence and me to put him to rest, without ceremony, but with honest regret and sorrow. Listening to the pompous minister sing Celine's praises made me ill, and another glance at the man I supposed was Juan showed me that he, too, was disgusted with the hypocrisy of such *pro forma* praise. He knew better than anyone, perhaps best of all, that Celine had been possessed by the devil. *Had he,* I wondered, *ridden the horse that Nash followed from the site of the killing to the ranch?* There was that in his face that told me such a thing was possible — that granite determination, a barely hidden conscious pride in his own strength and judgment passed down through generations. If, indeed, Nash had discovered the truth and kept it hidden, it was because he recognized himself in the old man — saw and respected another lion's courage.

Would Juan or one of the others speak? I watched him struggle with himself, lips trembling, his large hands clenched, the knuckles white.

Don't! I wanted to shout. *Not now!* — and was relieved when the dragging eulogy ended and Godbolt stepped forward unsteadily and placed one red rose on the coffin before it was lowered into the ground. He bent and tossed in the first handful of dirt before turning away, and it seemed he had aged years in only a few weeks. Nash Fallon, of all people, took his elbow, sensing that the man was barely capable of walking.

A dry, hot wind had sprung up out of nowhere, and a dust devil formed, danced its mad dance up the hill away from us. I thought it was an omen — a manifestation of the mischievous gods reminding us that we were all merely spinning tops in the hands of fate.

The crowd slowly dispersed, moved disjointedly back down the hill. I watched Juan, his hand in the hand of the servant girl, who looked at me with concern. He, however, paid me no attention, and I was grateful.

Silently I cursed secrecy. I have always detested innuendo as merely an evasive form of untruth. I was sick of it all — especially the way truth seemed to be almost in our hands, only to have another loose end show itself. Those who knew spoke only in hints. Even the servant girl, who had told me so much, probably knew more. But these were cautious people, and she had no reason to trust me. I was, after all, a *gringa,* and the old fears, the old hatreds still lived.

The country seemed cursed with an evil

that rose up out of the ground like a disease that infected all of us — women, children, Mexicans, whites, even Stefan and me talking our endless circle.

"Unbelievable," I muttered.

"What is?" Lawrence had caught up with me.

"Let's get out of here. I'll tell you on the way home where we're sure no one will overhear us, or watch us and suspect we're plotting against them whether we are or not."

"It won't be the first time," Lawrence said. "I read somewhere that up in Wyoming in the Johnson County Range War talking against the other side was an offense that could get you killed. It's always the same when the power hungry try to take over everything."

Saying — "Let's get out of here." — was becoming a bad habit. Nothing anywhere, and especially here at Godbolt's *hacienda* fortress, was what it seemed. My theory of masks was evolving day by day, and I was heartily sick of it.

We cleared the *hacienda*'s gates and turned east. With a sense of relief, I untied my bonnet and fanned my face. The day had turned hot, and dust from the horses' hoofs rose in our faces.

"Glad to be out of there?" Lawrence asked, lifting one eyebrow.

"You don't know how glad. What did Briscoe tell you? Does Godbolt know about María?"

He shook his head. "No. Briscoe probably knows, though. He had something mighty serious on his mind that he wasn't letting out to me. I sure wasn't about to do his job for him and tell the colonel. Not after how he looked at the cemetery. Even if he is a murderous old devil, you had to feel sorry for him."

"That old man was Juan, I think," I said then. "And to complicate matters, he was María's father."

Lawrence's jaw dropped. "Jesus! No wonder he looked the way he did. Like he was ready to commit mass murder. Poor old guy. He's in a real bind, if you want to talk about motive. And here I was thinking I'd learned a lot from Briscoe."

"What *did* you learn?"

"Godbolt sent for María and the boy to come back for the funeral. That's why he had delayed it so long. He can't understand why he hasn't got word from the girl, but nobody's got the guts to tell him. I'm almost positive that Trig told Briscoe who the girl was. Looks like he's trying to figure out how

169

to handle Godbolt and still keep his own head on. Godbolt is convinced Jacky Chastain killed Celine and has offered a five thousand dollar reward for him. We'll have to protect him more than ever . . . if he even comes back. The other thing . . . I got the feeling Briscoe's not too happy to be involved in all this killing, but he's in too deep and doesn't know how to get out. He probably remembers what happened to Sheriff Brady down in Lincoln County."

Billy the Kid and his friends had shot the sheriff down in the street of Lincoln in revenge for the killing of John Tunstall by Brady's deputies. The same thing could, I thought, happen in Lost River where the sheriff was either unwilling or unable to uphold the law.

"A lot of people around here have a motive to even the score with Briscoe, and I think he knows it," Lawrence said. "With that in mind, I've sent out a few more telegrams that may get us some help. I just hope it gets here in time."

"To whom now?" I was curious and interested in this statement, hoping it meant that we weren't about to pull out.

"To my father for one. He has connections."

That was an understatement. I had no

idea which connection Haslett, Sr., would tap, but I knew he could go right to the top in Washington, if need be.

We were coming up on the ruins of the Chastain ranch when, in the distance, I saw a familiar figure — a man leading a laden burro, and walking slowly. Any further chance to discuss the discoveries we'd made was cut off for the time being.

"It's Stefan!" I cried, unable to conceal my delight, and Lawrence turned to look at me in surprise. Fortunately he had no time to inquire why I seemed so glad to see the priest, for we pulled alongside, and I moved over to make room.

CHAPTER NINETEEN

"My prayer has been answered." Stefan groaned as he tied the burro to the back and climbed up on the seat. "I wasn't sure I could walk another mile."

"I thought you were used to it." I spoke lightly, but was appalled at how he looked, his brown robe dust-covered, his face set in lines of pain and exhaustion.

"A thorn in the foot makes a difference."

He was wearing sandals, and his right foot was bound with a grimy rag.

"When we get back, I'll take care of that,"

I said, disguising my fear of infection and all that went with it.

"That would be good."

He closed his eyes, and I sneaked another look at him. In repose his face belonged to another, simpler man, perhaps the man he had been once, a long time before.

"What do you see, Sidra?" He turned and impaled me with a glance.

"A very tired man."

"And you will minister to my needs." His statement carried what I heard as a not-too-subtle message.

I accepted his challenge. "Yes," I said. "Somebody has to."

Beside me, Lawrence seemed uneasy, as if he sensed the undercurrents between us. "We're almost there," he said.

"Why are you all not working?" Stefan adroitly changed the subject. "I didn't think you took pleasure rides or went on picnics."

"The valley's gone to hell in a hand cart while you were gone, if you'll excuse the expression. Tell him, Sidra. I'm not sure where to start."

I did, watching sadness slowly film those brilliant eyes. I told him what Lawrence had heard at the funeral, that the colonel believed Jacky had killed Celine and had offered a reward for his capture.

"So we only thought the devil was loose," he said when I'd finished. "Now we'll find out what he does in his wrath."

"You sound like an Old Testament prophet."

"There are worse things."

"Are your prophesies always right?"

He laughed. "Hardly ever. But I'll pray that Jacky is safe, and that he comes back to us. And to do my part, I'll go to visit the colonel. Maybe I can convince him the boy isn't to blame."

"Oh, sure. And maybe you can raise the dead."

"Sarcasm doesn't become you, Sidra. Especially when you know better. I hope I can put the dead to rest and save the people in this valley."

It was a slap on the wrist, and, coming from him, it hurt. I clenched my hands in my lap and didn't answer, making him laugh again.

"Don't pout," he said.

I made no response to that, either, and it was with relief that I saw our camp just as we'd left it.

Someone, probably at Godbolt's order, had loaded our wagon with food from the wake. There was a washtub of barbecue, fried chicken, biscuits, and several watermelons wrapped in canvas.

"A feast for the gods." Stefan was chewing on a chicken leg, his energy restored. "My poor Indians wouldn't believe their eyes. Or their stomachs."

I supposed he was always thinking of the poor who made up the greater part of his flock. While I had been as poor as any, I'd always had enough to eat, unlike the two children I'd seen inspecting our food package only the day before. At the recollection, I said: "Mercy Fellows and her kids are camped down by the river. Yesterday we took them food. I think I'll take them some of this, too. I'll take another basket to them in the morning."

"I'll go with you."

"No." I shook my head. "You'll stay off that foot. I'm sure Lawrence will put you to work sitting down."

"I will. We're so far behind what I'd hoped, we'll be lucky to get down to the bottom level before snow flies. So far, all we've had is disaster." Lawrence got up and dusted his hands. "I've got a hunch it's not going to get better, either."

"Let's for once not talk about it." I stood, too, and beckoned to Stefan. "Let me take a look at your foot while it's still light."

"Like Magdalene," he said, smiling.

"Not hardly."

"A pity." Again he was challenging me.

Ignoring him, I went to my wagon and opened my medicine chest. Magdalene, indeed! But I had to face what was an obvious attraction, and, even worse, he, too was aware of it. When I collected what I wanted, I went out and found him sitting on a boulder.

"Don't make fun of me," I said.

"I wouldn't."

"You just did."

"It was an allegory. But not making fun."

"Next you'll ask me to let down my hair."

"Why not?" He was still smiling. "They say hair is a woman's crowning glory and you have beautiful hair."

I bent and removed his sandal. The wound was clean but raw, aggravated by miles of walking across rough and inhospitable country. His foot was warm and somehow trusting in my hands. I'd never washed anyone's feet but my own, not even Edward's, and the act itself seemed holy, as if we were both being blessed, as if I held not an extremity but a beating heart.

Perhaps Magdalene, too, had felt like this at the feet of Jesus — respectful, overcome with compassion for mortality — His and her own.

"You should wear boots." I placed his foot in a basin of water, seeking refuge in practicality. "You should take care of yourself. If you had boots, this wouldn't have happened."

"My boots wore out. You tell me how to find a shoemaker in the desert. And you changed the subject."

Of course, I had. "You're a priest. I know that even if you want to deny it."

"I'm a man who appreciates beauty when I find it. And I'm a man who speaks his mind."

"As you please, but sometimes I'd rather you didn't." Carefully I dried his callused foot and took it in my lap to bandage it.

"Why not? It's not often I meet a beautiful and talented woman. In fact, I can't remember if I ever did. Imagine my life, if you can. Days, months, years spent talking to myself or to God. That's how I learned to say what I think. There's no hiding it . . . from either of us. Imagine the confessions I hear. The same petty sins over and over, the same simple souls asking forgiveness, and who am I to forgive them when I'm as big a sinner as they are?"

"You're not. How can you say that?" I was forced to come to his defense, having always believed that priests, ministers, were un-blemished, an innocent belief, but I'd never had to examine it closely.

He reached out and cupped my chin in one hand. "Look at me. I told you once before, I am a man as well as priest. And like any man, both good and bad. My demons are like anyone else's, even yours. After I left here, I thought about you. Your kindness, your intelligence, your capable ways, that passion in you . . . for work, for life, for me . . . though you think you hide it. But not from me."

I wrenched my chin away. No one, man or woman, had ever spoken to me like this. No one had ever seen me as I was and am. Though I had lain with Edward, and had tasted something of passion — or lust — with Nash, always I had kept a piece of myself intact, always I had been in posses-sion of that place — call it nucleus, core, center of being — that had been mine alone, and sacred.

"I don't want to hear!" I buried my face in my hands so I wouldn't have to see him. The basin of water spilled into my lap, but I hardly noticed, kneeling there stripped naked, not of clothing but of all my puny protection. Nash, too, had sensed my vulnerability and done something about it — almost.

Stefan put a hand on my head. It felt like a blessing, but I refused it.

"Sidra." His voice was deep with a hint of that humor so much a part of him. "Sidra, there's nothing wrong with being who you are, feeling what you feel. I've just admitted to being human. Why should you be different?"

Why, indeed? Was it because I was a woman and defenseless? I dropped my hands and looked up, saw his face with its lines and furrows, saw sadness there and that all-compelling radiance in his eyes.

"Because," I whispered.

"A splendid answer. From a schoolgirl. One I wouldn't have expected from you. But don't be afraid, Sidra. The choice is yours."

"So I can damn us both? So I can play Eve to your wide-eyed Adam?" I sounded bitter, even to myself.

He shook his robes down around his ankles and sighed. "You think too much."

"For a woman, you mean," I said, anger battling my insight into the soul of a thwarted male.

He laughed. "Much better than 'because' as an answer, and typical. Now finish your doctoring and let me go say my prayers. I'll pray that we exorcise our demons and stay friends."

Just like that, I thought. *Just like that he casts me out. Before I'm allowed time to change my mind.* Shocked at my own admission of hypocrisy, I concentrated on applying salve to the place where the thorn had pierced deeply into his flesh. Then I bandaged it.

When I finished, I packed up the medicine and the empty bowl and left without another word. Looking back, I saw him, a solitary figure, head bowed as if in prayer.

Above and around him swallows swooped and cried their shrill cries, a hundred slim, swift bodies like kites or the souls of the damned, slicing the night air.

For a long time I lay on my bed, wide-awake, too confused for tears or sleep. I heard the men around the fire talking in low tones, and, beyond them, the fluting call of the lesser nighthawk, tremulous, seeking, sweet as honey. It seemed to me to be the sound of my heart, a lonely questing for impossibility.

A while later, I heard a rustling at my door and sat up, clutching the blanket to my throat. "Who is it?"

"Me." Jacky slipped inside, then peered out into the night.

"Where have you been? Did anybody see you come back?"

"Don't think so. I gave a bunch of 'em the slip. I sneaked down under the overhang. Is there anything to eat?"

"First tell me where you've been."

"Hidin' out with friends that I know ain't apt to turn me over to the sheriff like *him.*"

That hurt, but he had a right to feel that way. I could hardly forget my conversation with Lawrence over whether my new son had killed Celine. There were others with better motives, probably some we didn't even know, but it was not impossible that, in his anger and sorrow, Jacky had taken revenge.

"We aren't going to turn you over to anyone. If you believe that, why did you come back?"

"They was burned out and maybe killed just like my folks. Last night. We all run and scattered. I couldn't find them, so I came back here."

With Celine not yet in the ground, Godbolt had turned loose his evil legions. Had Nash been with them? If he had been, he'd used up a horse getting back in time for the funeral. All in all, it had been a busy week for Mr. Fallon, I thought.

Obviously, however, this wasn't the time to press Jacky for further details. I was sure he'd tell me everything in time. "We have plenty to eat. Stay here and don't, for any reason, come out," I warned.

He sat down on his cot with what sounded like a sigh of complete exhaustion, and I could only imagine what he'd been through.

"There's water in the pitcher to wash with," I told him. "And drinking water in the canteen. I'll be right back."

In robe and boots, I crept out and over to the kitchen, where I loaded a plate and, at the last, tucked a small melon under my arm, all achieved, miraculously, in darkness.

"What are you doing?" The voice came out of nowhere, and I gasped and dropped the melon that burst open on my foot.

"What are *you* doing? Creeping around like a shadow! You scared the daylights out of me."

Stefan chuckled. "I couldn't sleep, so I came out to look at the stars and found you."

"Jacky's in my wagon."

"And wanting food, no doubt. A good sign."

I stepped over the remains of the melon.

"I guess boys are always hungry."

"Men, too."

Ignoring the dual implications of that, I said: "Come on. He'll be glad to see you."

Together we crowded into the wagon, found Jacky stretched out on the bed in an exhausted asleep. He didn't even stir.

"Should we wake him?" I whispered.

"Let him sleep. God knows he probably needs it. Just make sure he doesn't show himself in the morning."

"He told me he was chased here and gave them the slip. Someone burned out whoever he'd been hiding out with. There are probably men on the cliff watching us right now."

"No doubt wanting the reward. If I could think of a way, I'd take him to the mission. He'd be safe there."

And where would I be safe? Where would I be happy? Perhaps there was no haven for me, no place of belonging.

I left the food on the shelf and we stepped down from the wagon. Overhead, the night sky burned with millions of stars and the spill of the Milky Way, and somewhere a mockingbird was going through his repertoire, never repeating himself, singing, I thought, from pure happiness.

Without warning, Stefan put his arms around me. His breath was fast and warm on my cheek as he drew me close. "Sidra . . . Sidra . . . ," he said in the moment before he kissed me.

And I? My response was instant — a flame, an explosion like a shooting star. In that moment nothing mattered, not death, not Nash, not the threat of damnation.

"I . . . you. . . ." The words wouldn't come, but even if they had, they'd have been cut short.

In the distance, reverberating off the stone face of the mountain, we heard the thunder of galloping horses. When the sound faded, and the night silence had closed around us again, the moment had passed.

"Night riders . . . it's started," was all he said.

CHAPTER TWENTY

"Missus!" Jacky's urgent call startled me out of a deep sleep.

"What?"

"It's light already and I gotta go out."

"You can't." I shoved the chamber pot at him. "Use this. Call me when you're through."

I climbed outside, wondering what had happened to his wish to call me ma, then remembered my joy of the night before — a joy cut off too soon — replaced by terror. *Night riders*. The very words evoked danger — hoofs striking sparks in the dark, masked men bent on death and destruction, no different from the Klu Klux Klan that even now still terrorized the South.

I looked up and made what I hoped was a careless survey of the cliffs. It was not light enough for anyone up there to see me, even with field glasses, but caution was becoming second nature. All I saw was a sky dappled with small clouds, a hawk circling in search of breakfast.

The sun hadn't yet breached the eastern barrier. It was that hour when the sky still held a purple hint of night and when the western mountains burned crimson as if lit by an inner fire. Somewhere up the cañon, a wren greeted the morning with its sweet and unmistakable song, and the mockingbird, still awake and in splendid voice, mimicked it.

It was a moment of incredible beauty, marred by the fact that somewhere in the valley homes had been ruthlessly destroyed, lives brought to an abrupt and vicious end.

Human nature is a vile and obscene thing when compared to the other handiwork of God. Unhappily, there is little or nothing that can be done to improve it. Godbolt, I realized, was only one of many monsters, his kingdom a minute dot on the map of the world.

"Psst!" Jacky hissed at me.

"Stay where you are."

"Am I gonna have to sit in here all day?" He sounded cranky, like he'd reached the end of his rope, and I couldn't blame him.

"We'll figure something out," I said. "But until then, yes. I'll go bring you breakfast."

Dan took one look at me in my robe, my bare feet shoved into melon-spattered boots, my hair still in its night-time braid, and, being funny, or at least trying to be, said: "Gosh, Sidra, what'll people think?"

"Whatever they want, as usual." I wasn't in a playful mood. "We've got a new problem, and it's not about my appearance."

"Well," Lawrence said when I'd told them about Jacky and the men who had followed him, "then he can't stay here!"

For once I agreed with him, not that I thought we shouldn't fight for him if we had to. "Brilliant deduction, Doctor Watson! What do you propose we do instead?"

My sarcasm hit a sore spot, and he straightened to his arrogant best. "That's enough, Sidra."

I opened my mouth, then shut it when Stefan stepped between us.

185

"Fighting among ourselves will get us nowhere. When night comes, I'll take Jacky up to a cave that has a spring in it, and I'll vouch no one knows about it. If I thought I could take the boy away, I'd do it, but Godbolt's men will be everywhere. We wouldn't get five miles in the daytime, and, if we tried it at night, they'd pick up our trail the next day and follow like the hounds of hell. For now, we go about our business. Sidra can go to Mercy's, and I'll sit by the wagon door, looking like a priest meditating, and keep Jacky entertained. The rest of you . . . go back to work."

It was a simple plan. Whether it would fool our watchers remained to be seen. I dressed in Lawrence's tent, then left on my errand, unsure of what I would find, or my reception at Mercy's hands this time, but determined to find out. I drove the light wagon we had used before, my .32-20 Winchester handy, my .41 Colt in my shoulder bag, and despite the danger, the complexity of my situation, I laughed as I thought: *If they could see me back home and know I'm armed to the teeth, the aunts and grannies would reach for the smelling salts.*

I decided I was less apt to get a load of buckshot from Mercy's shotgun if I approached with a clatter. I still wasn't certain

186

she had all her wits, nor was I sure that I wouldn't be met by her "army". Lawrence hadn't been wrong about the horse tracks. The trail looked like a herd of them had passed through not long before.

I drove right into camp and was met by Mercy, who for once wasn't pointing her shotgun at me, although it was leaning against the wagon wheel beside her. For the first time, she looked almost friendly. "What brings you here?"

"More grub," I said. "It isn't poisoned, either. We've been eating it. You'll think it's all the sweeter when I tell you we got it from the leftovers of the spread Godbolt laid out for Celine's funeral."

She looked surprised. "Say that again."

"Godbolt sent the leftovers home with the people who were at the funeral. There was more than enough for everyone."

She humphed at that. "Reckon the old bastard could afford it. How did he look knowin' his tribe got it this time, instead of some poor homesteader's family?"

"Terrible," I said. "He could hardly walk without help. It hit him hard."

"Good! Maybe it'll kill him."

I thought: *No such luck.*

"Anyhow, I've got a lot more stuff that you and the kids can use, I suspect." Then, trying her out a little, I said: "I see you've had a lot of visitors lately."

That hit her. She gave me a hard look. "You ain't as much a dude as I reckoned. Light and stretch yore legs."

I got down off the seat slowly. "Thanks. I've been in the West a few years. It rubs off on you."

She humphed again. "On some mebbe."

The kids came out of hiding, reminding me of shy animals, fawns, unused to people like me but curious.

I smiled at them. "Jacky told me the boy is Bucky, and who is this little one with all the curls?"

Mercy cackled. "Mercy. Named her for me, thinkin' she might grow up as good-lookin' as her maw. She still has a few years to work on it."

At least, I thought, she could still laugh, if the rusty sound that came out of her could be called that. But I had no more time to think about it. The sound of horses coming at a fast trot alerted both of us. The kids retreated again, like quail shooed by their mama, but Bucky grabbed his .22 before he left.

Mercy swung up her shotgun as two men wearing deputies' badges rode in. They looked us over with suspicion, especially me. I judged they hadn't expected to find me there, as proved to be the case.

I didn't like the looks of either of them, but the spokesman was particularly uncouth, with a heavy paunch, red, unshaven face, and long drooping mustache. He was chewing tobacco, and spit between me and Mercy. I stepped away from the brown mess, lifting my skirts in distaste. As I watched him, I became almost sure he'd been with the dead wagon the day I'd found Jacky, and I hated him then with a hint of that passion Stefan so admired.

He ignored me, focused on Mercy and her weapon. "You kin put the scatter-gun down, lady. We ain't gonna hurcha. Out on law business. We follered some tracks up here from where a ranch was burned out last night."

I thought: *I'll just bet you did. You're on Jacky's trail, or maybe the folks who owned the ranch that was burned out, most likely by you and your gang, and now you want to pin the blame on somebody else and finish the job.*

"Ain't seen a soul," Mercy said, never wavering with her scatter-gun or taking her eyes off the men.

"I said you can put up that gun now," the fat deputy repeated.

"And you can go to hell!" Mercy said. "I wouldn't trust you any further'n I could throw a hoss without coverin' you with Sweet Betsy here."

We were taken by surprise by a third deputy who stepped from behind the wagon. "Don't turn around, lady, or I'll perforate you so you won't hold coffee worth a damn."

I gave him credit for a colorful manner of speaking, but recognized him as the other man on the dead wagon. *Buzzard*, I thought. *Scavenger*, and almost choked on my own rage.

He slipped up, reached around Mercy, and jerked the shotgun out of her hands, then hit her with his six-shooter hard enough to stagger her, but she was tough and wiry and kept her feet. He sheathed his six-shooter and hefted the shotgun, looking smug, then turned vicious again.

"You old bitch. You tried to lie your old man out of the rope."

At that Mercy went berserk. She rushed him, and somehow wrenched the shotgun out of his hands. The fat deputy went for his six-shooter and yelled: "Get back! I'll shoot her."

He never had the chance. Bucky's .22 cracked, and we watched as he toppled from his horse.

"What the hell!" Distracted, the third man wasn't in time to escape Mercy's scatter-gun. The short range blast of buckshot threw him backward, and he fell to the ground.

The remaining deputy had his pistol out, and he was pointing it at Bucky who had come out of the brush, shouting: "I ain't got any more bullets!"

Mercy squeezed off a shot, but missed. That gave me my chance. Almost without realizing what I was doing, I had pulled out my .41, cocking it as I drew, aimed, and fired, just as Edward had taught me.

In books they tell you that properly bred ladies are supposed to swoon at a time like that, or feel revulsion, but, when I shot that man and saw him hit the ground, what I felt was victorious, proud of myself, relieved at having saved Mercy and Bucky. Most unfeminine of me, or perhaps not. Female animals will kill to protect their own, and, standing there, I realized Mercy was one of my own, one of the "little ones", as Stefan often called his Indians.

Mercy recovered first. "Good shootin'. You sure as hell ain't no prissy dude."

Only then did I begin to feel weak in the knees. I put my six-shooter back in my bag and leaned against the wagon, breathing hard.

Mercy reloaded her shotgun, then looked at me. "Be you all right? You done jist right and don't let it get you. They aimed to kill me and the kids, and then they'd've had to shoot you, too. You saved us all."

It was true. I had killed a man, for he certainly was dead. I'd shot him close to the heart.

All three were dead. The one Bucky shot had the now familiar hole in the forehead, the signature of the local crack shots.

Bucky said: "Don't you worry, lady. Like Ma said, you done jist right."

I noticed that his voice, like Mercy's, was surprisingly steady. Either they had become used to violence and killing, or they were tough as bull hide. Thinking it over, I decided a little bit of both.

When Mercy saw I wasn't going to get the vapors, she got practical. "You git the hell out of here fast, lady. There may be more of 'em. And remember, you never saw us. And we didn't see a thing. We'll take care of these three buzzards." She cackled her now familiar laugh. "I got my own dead wagon, you might say. Now git. And remember you came over and nobody was here, so you left the basket and went back. That's yore story

192

and be sure to stick to it, no matter what somebody tries to get out of you."

I drove back to camp a different woman. I was now a killer, and who could I tell? How could I admit to the rush of gratification that had swept me? That I'd had justification was the least of it. I thought it would be best to take Mercy's advice and not tell anyone, at least not until I'd had a chance to think about it. Lawrence would have a hissie if I told him. And Stefan? He carried a six-shooter, and had probably had worse things told to him in confession. If I ever confessed to anyone that I had killed a man, I thought it would be to him.

CHAPTER TWENTY-ONE

Stefan was at his post when I returned, probably keeping his promise to introduce Jacky to Greek mythology. He got up and held the team while I got down.

"That didn't take long."

I steeled myself. "Nobody was there. I left the basket and came back." Then I watched him to see if his acute lie detection sense set off an alarm, but he merely looked worried. I had, it seemed, become both an accomplished liar and killer all in one morning.

"I wonder where they are," he said. "Godbolt wouldn't hesitate killing women and children. And Mercy is a thorn in his side."

Jacky, who had been listening from his hiding place in the wagon, said: "And they'd have killed me, too. I'm gonna even the score for Ma and Pa if it's the last thing I do."

It was useless to reason with him about that, though getting even might be the last thing he ever did.

"Just keep out of sight or you might not be around to even the score," I told him. "There's a five thousand dollar reward on your head, and, if they see you down here, they'll come charging in like a cavalry troop."

He gaped at me. "A how much reward?" Obviously he hadn't heard that before.

"Five thousand dollars."

He whistled, then looked scared. "They'll be down on me like a duck on a June bug."

"We'll get you to a safe hideaway that I know about, tonight," Stefan reassured him. "It's a secret cave with a spring."

Stefan had used the word secret to make it more attractive. Jacky looked impressed, then another thought took hold of him. "If it's got a spring, it'll be crawlin' with snakes waitin' for rabbits and the like."

Stefan laughed. "I have an Indian friend who put a spell on the place so snakes would avoid it. I've never seen a one there."

Jacky looked skeptical. "Injuns can't make spells," he said.

"Wait and see. Have I ever lied to you?"

Whatever Jacky's answer, it was disrupted by distant gunfire, and the crew came running from the dig.

"Jesus!" Lawrence said. "It sounds like a skirmish line."

I wondered how he'd know what a skirmish line sounded like, but got my answer when he crossed over to his wagon and got out a long gun case. From it he withdrew a rifle that was different from the familiar frontier Winchesters. "Krag," he said. "A Thirty-Forty. It'll shoot a mile. I bought mine from the Army and brought it home from the war."

"What war?" I asked stupidly.

"Not the Civil War," he said. "Now let's spread out and get behind boulders." He pointed to which boulders he meant and swept his arm back and forth indicating those on the hillside above camp and opposite the direction of the gunfire. "I'll get

195

the horses down in the hollow and tie them. Move!"

He spoke in a new voice that I'd never heard. This was Captain Haslett of the Rough Riders as I would discover before the day was out, Captain Haslett, who had never once mentioned that he'd gone up San Juan Hill with Teddy Roosevelt.

Not all the Rough Riders had come from the West. Many had been recruited from the Ivy League and social registers in the East, at least one of the reasons that Lawrence had "influence" in high places. T.R. was then in as high a place as you could get in the U.S., and he had a standing rule that any Rough Rider had access to him in the White House anytime they paid a visit. Just now, however, we were on our own, and no one was more conscious of it than I. I'd killed once today, and might end up doing it again, or getting killed myself.

We took our positions, ten feet or more apart, behind boulders, as Lawrence had directed. Even Jacky grabbed his .22 and took a position, ready to protect and defend, and Dan, Hugh, and Scott came back with all the canteens of water they could pack. The peppering fire from down the cañon continued, then slowly tapered off.

Lawrence called out to us. "You all hold

your positions! I'm going to climb the hill to get a better view, and I'll stay up there to cover you from anyone across the cañon. I'll be within yelling distance, but keep quiet unless it's an emergency. If anyone we don't know shows up, I'm going to fire a warning shot to get rid of them or develop their intentions."

He hadn't forgotten about the men Jacky thought had followed him, nor did any of us have illusions about who was involved in gunfire, least of all me. Godbolt's men had jumped Mercy's camp, but her "army" had been hidden out nearby. I hoped they'd got the bodies buried, or at least out of sight. If not, Briscoe would be after Mercy for the murder of three deputies, one of whom had my bullet in him.

The firing finally stopped. We waited a while, but neither saw nor heard anything besides the birds and the stirring of a welcome breeze in the trees.

I heard the sound of a wagon at about the same time Lawrence yelled: "Wagons coming up the cañon!"

Since no one hostile would be coming in wagons, I was more curious than fearful, and stood up to watch. Mercy came first, with Bucky and his sister on either side of her.

In all, five wagons came into view with several horsemen riding beside them like a cavalry escort. They entered our campground and pulled up.

Only then did Lawrence yell down to us. "OK! You people can leave your positions and go see what's going on." Then he scrambled rapidly down the slope.

"What happened?" I asked Mercy as soon as I reached her.

She was grinning from ear to ear. "Some coyotes showed up down at our camp and got a big surprise. We had ourselves a leetle shoot-out and they skedaddled, but not before we emptied a few saddles. I reckon they thought nesters wouldn't put up a fight."

Some nesters, I thought. Probably half of them had been in the war with Lawrence. Anybody who could shoot a man off a moving horse was no novice, and, with a scatter-gun like Mercy's, you didn't even have to be a very good shot. I wondered if she'd added to her bag total for the day, but thought it better not to ask.

Lawrence's arrival broke up any further conversation. He had reverted to Professor Haslett. "What are you people doing here?" he demanded.

Mercy had taken his measure the day

before. "Free country, Doctor," she said. "We aim to fort up where there's water and high ground."

A stranger in her cavalcade edged up on his horse and looked Lawrence over with the ill-concealed distaste of a died-in-the-wool Westerner for someone from "back there". Some of these old-timers hated dudes so badly they wouldn't even say the word East, or Easterner.

"You got any objections?" he asked.

For once Lawrence didn't lose his red-head's temper. He shrugged. "It makes pretty good sense in view of what's been going on." He motioned back up the hill he'd just come down. "In fact, I'd post a couple of men up there all the time, day and night. Whoever has the longest range rifles."

At that, the man's belligerence moderated, and I was sure that was what Lawrence had intended. As Mercy had pointed out, this was a "free country". We couldn't run these people off, but we could join forces. In addition, there was a moral issue at stake — good against evil — and good needed all the help it could get.

"Why don't you find places to park your wagons in the shade?" Lawrence, used to being in command and obeyed, went on:

"We have an archeological dig going here to look for ancient Indian ruins, but you can see where we've staked it off. I'd appreciate your staying out of those areas." He had noticed several children in the group, and added: "And please keep the kids out of them."

By then most of the people had come up to hear what he was saying, and nodded their heads in agreement and probably in relief. Lawrence, as ever, was practical. "How do you people plan to get provisions? Unless I miss my guess, you'll have to fight your way into town."

Mercy pointed up the cañon. "The old road goes over the mountains to Hatch's Siding . . . it's below Sacaton on the railroad. It ain't much of a town, but it's got a general store."

After dispatching the two men up on the bluff under the cliffs, the rest of the newcomers set about pitching camps. Before she even got off her wagon, Mercy said to Lawrence: "Well, I reckon you got a helluva lot more common sense than I figured. We're much obliged."

At the unexpected compliment, Lawrence looked confused, then scratched his head and said the last thing I ever expected to hear. "Well, I'll be go to hell!"

When our laughter subsided, Stefan, his eyes twinkling, said: "I surely hope not, Doctor. I think I'll pray for you."

And that set us off again.

Later that afternoon, Trig showed up with Dr. Goldwater, the coroner, and it was a toss-up as to who was the more startled, the deputy or Mercy's group, most of whom grabbed for their weapons.

"What in hell are they doin' here?" Trig wanted to know. "You throwin' in with them?"

"I'll explain," Lawrence said, who'd been busy calming down Mercy and the others. "Make sure they all know what's going on," he said to her. "And we might need help bringing the bodies down."

As it happened, two husky fellows volunteered for the job, probably out of curiosity, but their faces, as they came down with their canvas-wrapped load, suggested they wished they'd contained their curiosity. Even I moved as far away as I could from the stink of the decomposed bodies, and I made sure I was upwind when Goldwater began his examination.

"Jeezuz! Someone did a real job on her!" Goldwater looked around and said to Lawrence: "I'll have to swear in you and your party as a coroner's jury."

He didn't have to explain why. In God-bolt's country no one would have accepted the decision of a nester coroner's jury even if it were sworn on a stack of Bibles. A nester's word went about as far as an Indian's or Mexican's in some communities.

I wondered if Goldwater knew the dead girl's name. If I got a chance, I intended to get Trig alone and find out which way the wind was apt to blow now. He'd looked at Lawrence a couple of times as though he'd like to have a private word with him, and I called that to Lawrence's attention.

He nodded. "I noticed. All in good time. They aren't going to go back in the dark. We'll have plenty of time later."

"Do you think he told the sheriff?"

"I thought so, but now I doubt it. If he did, the sheriff would be with him. Although Briscoe sure had something on his mind at the funeral."

After Goldwater's examination was finished, the question of what to do with the bodies had to be settled. "Bury 'em here," Goldwater said. "Nobody knows who they are."

I let myself relax a little. If the coroner didn't know, neither did Briscoe nor Godbolt, who would have redoubled his violence.

"Let's bury them up there under the juniper," I suggested. That way Joe Chastain would have some company.

"Wherever." Goldwater was more concerned with getting the corpses in the ground, the sooner the better. He recruited his volunteers to dig the grave, which they were more than willing to do when they found out he was authorized to pay them.

To Stefan, Goldwater said: "Glad you're here, Father. We can do this up all right and proper. And the county can make a little donation to the parish in the bargain. For your Injuns," he added.

Stefan grinned. "Bless you . . . and the county, of course."

Goldwater looked at me. "I understand you're a photographer just like the *padre* here. You wouldn't have one of them newfangled little cameras to get some pictures for the record?"

For a moment I wondered if he knew of my other incriminating photographs, but I nodded assent. "A Kodak," I said, "and I'd be glad to do it."

"We'll pay the going rate."

Goodness! Every time I turned around, someone was paying me! By the time we were finished at the dig, I'd have enough to tide me over for quite a while.

At the graveside, Mercy surprised us all by placing a little bouquet of wild flowers on the bodies, and I was even more surprised to see Trig remove the medallion from his pocket and place it on María's chest. "It was hers," he said, looking embarrassed. "She probably set a lot of store by it."

I took my pictures then, including a good one of her hands crossed on her bosom, holding the medallion, since there was no way we could have put it around what was left of her neck. I almost cried at the sight of her ruined face and matted hair that I knew had once been beautiful, her "crowning glory", as Stefan had commented of women's hair.

Stefan's ceremony was a model of what one should be, especially when I recalled the interminable tribute to Celine by the minister who had known nothing about her except that her father had a lot of money and who had put on a show to earn as much of it as possible.

Stefan held his crucifix in both hands and turned his face to heaven. For at least a minute, he prayed silently, and we stood quietly, praying each in our own way, spellbound by the aura that seemed to surround him — the priest, man of God.

He looked at each of us before beginning to speak in that musical voice that always thrilled me. "Father, we are here to commend two souls to Your mercy. They died alone and perhaps in terror and agony. We offer our love and pity for them even as we know You do. And we pray their souls are with You in heaven. . . . Amen."

The mourners stood open-mouthed. Most of them had come from the shouting Methodist or Baptist tradition of camp meetings and were used to — even expected — a long, emotional harangue.

I heard a man ask someone, probably his wife: "Is that all he aims to say?"

And I was satisfied when she answered. "It was enough."

Stefan made the sign of the cross over the bodies and sprinkled holy water over the canvas shrouds. I was struck by the aura that surrounded him, the dignity with which he carried himself, the absolute purity of his profile, so like the rugged cliffs behind him.

In that moment I accepted the fact that I loved him — priest and man. In that moment I realized I had never before loved anyone at all.

■ ■ ■ ■

It was night before I managed to be alone with Lawrence. I had seen him head to head with Trig but had been too astonished at the force of my own feelings to want to listen in.

"Well?" I asked.

"He didn't tell the sheriff. To quote him as best I can . . . and I'm getting rather good at it, if I do say so . . . he said . . . 'It's none of his damned business. I'm gonna go raise me some chickens. That girl deserved a lot better, and I hope the sky pilot had it right. I hope to hell she's in heaven. The kid, too.' "

Well said, I thought. *Damned well said.*

Then Lawrence turned my world upside down. "We're packing out of here in the morning."

"Now? You can't!" I couldn't keep the emotion out of my voice.

"The dig will be waiting for us after all the trouble blows over. We'll have to spend a couple of days in town, then I'm going back to Washington. The Smithsonian will have to make the best of it."

Stefan, in that soundless way of his, had come up to us and overheard. "I'll miss

206

you," he said, looking at me. To Lawrence he said, with a slight smile: "And if the Smithsonian wants to send someone in your place, tell them to bring Thirty-Forty's. What are your plans about the boy?"

"The boy" was sound asleep. He was tough, but the past weeks had taken a lot out of him. I knew, since it had drained me so that some days I was almost too tired to eat after having prepared the meals.

"He comes with me," I said. "No matter what, I'm adopting him."

Lawrence sighed. "We can't take Jacky to town with us. The sheriff would arrest him, take the five thousand . . . or somebody would, and then Jacky would disappear."

He was right, of course, but in five minutes the world had changed again, and I was leaving everyone I cared about, possibly forever.

"Then I will keep him," Stefan said. "No one will find him, and, when it's safe, I will take him with me to the mission. There my Injuns will see that no one gets him. You can come for him later, Sidra. Or I'll bring him to you."

I knew he was attempting a joke to make me feel better in his use of the localism, "Injuns". The tender gleam in his eye as he said it gave him away, and did me no good whatsoever.

Were all priests like him — humorous, compassionate, wise? Given human nature, I doubted it, and, remembering the steely strength of his arms around me, knew he wasn't typical. As he'd said: "I am also a man."

And I was a woman.

"I'll stay with you," I offered, torn by the thought of leaving him.

"No, you won't," Lawrence said. "I'm going to need you. I've already arranged for room and board in town and a place for you to photograph our artifacts before I pack them for shipment."

"You have been a busy beaver." I couldn't keep disappointment and sarcasm out of my voice. "Just how did you manage all this from out here?"

"I hired the sheriff the other day. He may be Godbolt's man, but he's up for odd jobs so long as they pay. By now he probably even has a hundred rolls or so of film for your Kodak."

"You planned this all along, is that what you're saying?"

"More or less. The trouble just pushed ahead my schedule by a few days. This is no place for us to be in. This isn't our war, and we're not going to fight in it."

Stefan looked as though he'd like to give Lawrence a lecture, but I took the job off his hands. "Then why'd you let those people in here? Why'd you give them hope? Fighting wrong, injustice, and evil is everyone's war! I know that if you don't."

"Amen!" Stefan said.

Lawrence didn't take offense. "No argument. But I've been in one too many wars. It's someone else's turn. I'm going to bed. See you in the morning. Don't get me up early. I'm worn out."

"War . . . of any kind . . . wears even the strongest down," Stefan said. "Still, I belong here and will keep fighting. But for now, I, too, am going to bed." With a bow to both of us, he walked into the night.

I wanted to run after him, to weep in his arms, but stayed where I was. He, after all, had chosen to leave me for reasons of his own, and I respected those reasons much as I deplored them.

What comfort I got came from anger at Lawrence. He'd brought me here and now was taking me away against my inclination and my will. Unfortunately he was also paying me, and I needed all the money I could get.

With a sigh, I went into my tent and slipped into bed, trying not to wake up

Jacky. I had no worry there. He was snoring, deep in that sleep from which we get our best rest. I doubted I'd sleep as well, if at all.

No troublesome moralizing about having become a "gunslinger" disturbed my mind. I'd done what was needed at the time, and had no regrets. Nor did I feel guilty that I kept seeing Stefan's lively eyes with their charming touch of self-mockery, the change in them when he'd surrendered to passion. I had met his passion without shame. Love comes where it will, and is, as he'd said, a gift from God. If so, this between us seemed an unlikely gift. I had heard of priests leaving their calling, but had no idea what Stefan intended. The way things were happening, I couldn't even decide what I was going to do. For the moment, all I could do was wish — and pray.

The birds were filling the air with their morning chorus when I finally opened my eyes. The sun had been up for a long while and I could smell coffee and the tantalizing odor of bacon frying. Jacky was still sound asleep.

I smiled at the sight of his tousled head resting on one arm, a little smile on his face. I wondered what he was dreaming. Maybe that his little horse, Poco, had come back. I wished that for him, too.

CHAPTER TWENTY-TWO

It was noon by the time everything was packed to Lawrence's satisfaction, so I prepared something to eat before we pulled out. Jacky had stayed beside me all morning, and I suspected he felt just as lost as I did.

Before I got in the wagon, I reached out and hugged him. "Don't forget I'm your new ma," I whispered. "I'll find you at Father Stefan's mission or meet you somewhere as soon as all this is over. I'll stay in touch with you both, and remember . . . I keep my promises."

His face was hidden against my breast, but I heard him murmur, " 'Bye, Ma. And . . . and please don't get killed like my other Ma."

"I won't," I said, and dropped a kiss on his head. "I won't, and that's a promise, too."

And then it was Stefan's turn. I stood there miserable, my heart in my eyes, and, as always, he understood, and opened his arms. "I don't want to go," I said. "To leave you."

"Only for a little while." With a gentle finger he wiped a tear away. "Don't cry, Sidra. My prayers and thoughts will go with you."

What good are prayers and thoughts? I wanted to say. *What good is anything if we're apart? When we might all be killed and for no good reason?* Instead, I kept silent, prolonging his embrace until I knew the others would notice and surely remark on it. I was being torn in half, my fears, my loyalties, my love all at war within.

"I love you," I whispered, and meant it. I was tired of pretense, sick of hiding myself, evading truth like a foolish schoolgirl.

His arms tightened. On his face, in those magnificent eyes, I read hope, determination, admiration, and something like despair. The choice was now his — a choice between a vow to God and love for me. Slowly he bent and kissed my cheek.

"Sidra!" Lawrence was becoming impatient — and, judging from his tone — perhaps a little jealous at what he couldn't understand.

"Coming!" I straightened my hat, lifted a hand to Stefan's cheek, then turned and ran.

All the way down the cañon I waved good bye to them, standing side-by-side, Stefan's hand on Jacky's shoulder. Then I prayed as

I'd never prayed before. *Please, God, keep them safe. Keep them safe.*

We rode a while in silence, I because I was unhappy and still angry at Lawrence who, in that high-handed way of his, had once again determined my future, and he because, just possibly, he was pondering the farewell he'd witnessed. I hoped that was so. I hoped he was jealous, though I'd never seen Lawrence any more interested in me than I was in him.

As we approached Mercy's old campsite, a wagon crossed the road about a quarter of a mile ahead of us, and Lawrence gestured at it.

"Guess we don't have to ask what that is."

I recognized those high board sides and lumbering wheels. "It looks like the dead wagon."

"What else? Only this time they're most likely picking up their own kind."

Yes, I thought with some satisfaction, *they probably are, but this time the original drivers are probably in it, not driving it.* It came home to me that I was now set apart from other humans. Most people never kill anyone, not because they wouldn't, but because they don't have to. I had to. I smiled grimly and hoped Lawrence didn't notice. Somewhere

I'd heard that those like Fallon developed a taste for killing. Certainly Mercy had no qualms about it — nor did Bucky. I wondered if, in the future, I, too, would develop the taste, become as hardened as Mercy and some of the others.

The wagon went on out of sight, but a lone rider, following it, paused in the road, apparently waiting for us. As we drew a little closer, I recognized Nash. He was not riding his big black or I'd have known who it was at once, and I hoped nothing had happened to it.

Lawrence drew up alongside him, and Fallon tipped his hat to me.

" 'Afternoon," he said in his Texas drawl.

Even after what had just transpired with Stefan, I felt the attraction of the man and as always marveled at his good looks.

" 'Afternoon," Lawrence replied.

"I reckon you're pullin' out," he observed, drawing his conclusion from the fact that all three of our wagons were on the road.

"I thought it best," Lawrence said. "For now, anyhow."

Fallon nodded. "Dangerous country. Somebody ambushed some of our cowboys yesterday." He looked dead serious, but had to be laughing inside at his brash lie.

"Were they unarmed?" Lawrence asked,

being equally droll and keeping a straight face.

"Everyone with good sense goes armed in this country."

Lawrence nodded agreement. "We heard shooting, but thought it best to mind our own business."

Fallon nodded in agreement. "A good rule anywhere."

I'm not sure what prompted Lawrence's next ploy, but he said: "I always wondered why you people carry those old-fashioned knuckle-buster pistols, if you'll pardon my prying. It seems to me that automatics shoot a lot faster and carry more loads."

Fallon thought that over. "I'm not so sure they're faster if you know what you're doing with one."

It was obvious that he carried two, and I'd bet he was as fast as anyone with one.

"I'm from Missouri," Lawrence said.

Nash grinned. "I'll show you, then, if you've got a minute to spare."

Without waiting for a reply, he was dismounting. Lawrence handed me the reins. "Hold the horses. And be ready if the shooting spooks them."

"Let's go over here on the side of the hill." Nash said, leading the way. "See that rock." He pointed at one about six inches in diameter, then backed away some twenty-five feet. He drew his right hand pistol and handed it to Lawrence. "Take out all but three rounds." It was a trick to find out if Lawrence knew how to operate an old single-action .45.

Lawrence obliged, and handed it back. "Now what?"

Nash whipped up the pistol, seemingly without aiming. I heard only one shot, and wondered what he'd wanted with three until I realized I'd seen the rock struck three times almost faster than my eye could register the sight.

Nash was enjoying himself. He handed the pistol to Lawrence and said: "Shuck 'em out. That was three shots."

He did as he was told, and Nash deliberately reloaded. "Want to try it?"

"I'm not much of a pistol shot."

"How about a rifle?"

"Better at that."

Nash drew a Winchester from his saddle boot and pointed up the hill. "Watch that boulder out there." It was at least a hundred yards away. He drove three rapid shots into the center. "Want to try that?"

Nash wasn't, I realized, simply showing off. He was conveying a message, a warning. What I was watching was a kind of struggle for power between two dominant and very powerful males.

Lawrence said: "Would you mind if I used my own rifle?"

"Go ahead."

He fished out his .30-40. Nash took a good look at it, but said nothing. Lawrence planted his feet like he was on a target range, pulled up, aimed briefly, and rapidly fired five shots, all of which could plainly be seen hitting within a few inches of each other at the center of the boulder.

I awarded him the blue ribbon for scoring one for himself and our side.

Nash said nothing, simply remounted, waved to his riders who had appeared at the sound of gunfire, tipped his hat to me again, and galloped off. At the top of the rise he turned and saluted us.

"What was that all about?" I asked Lawrence, wanting to hear Lawrence's explanation.

"War, or maybe poker," he said.

"Who won?"

"Hard to say. He's greased lightning. I'd like to know how he did that. He was fanning the gun, but most people fanning can't hit the broadside of a barn."

"I'll bet he wondered where you learned to shoot a rifle, too."

"I doubt it. It just came back to me where I'd seen him before. He's not easy to forget. He was in C Company. I was commander of A. He's bound to have known who I was all along."

"In the Rough Riders?"

"Sure. Teddy loved Texas gunslingers."

He drove on in silence, and I was content to be left to my thoughts. One of them was: *Neither one of them would believe that I'm a gunslinger, too.*

In town Lawrence drove directly to a corral next to a high, cut-stone building.

"What are we going to do here?" I asked.

"Live," he said. "It's our new home for a while. Used to be a flour mill. The owner had living quarters on the second floor. So we move in."

That didn't leave much to say. At least the place seemed to be in an excellent state of repair. "Does it have a kitchen?"

"Happens it does. And even has water pumped in. But if you don't feel like being cook and bottle washer any more, we can eat at a restaurant."

I remembered that the one at the Oriental Hotel had been surprisingly good. Without Jacky to help, the idea appealed to me.

"You've got a customer. I'll cook for holidays."

I expected to be back in Albuquerque before the next holiday — if I survived. I hadn't forgotten that Godbolt knew of my camera. If law and order ever came to Lost River, I could be a dangerous witness. It seemed to me Lawrence had simply moved us out of the frying pan into the fire.

By the time we'd unloaded everything, it was almost dark. In spite of the fact that we'd left the dig months earlier than intended, there was quite a stack of boxes and baskets, each one filled with artifacts.

Lawrence mopped his face and studied the now orderly pile. "The people here probably don't know this stuff will bring prices like diamonds with the right collectors, so let's not mention it."

"From Italian paintings and statues to broken pots," I said. "Quite a jump."

"But it's ours. It's our American art form, and it's been unappreciated until now. Still is, in a way. Let's clean up and go to dinner."

I was more than ready. The day had seemed like four, and the thought that I could put on a decent dress and be served a dinner I hadn't cooked was appealing.

"Duff! Duff Henley!"

At Lawrence's shout, the big man who'd been reading the newspaper in the lobby of the Oriental unfolded himself and stood.

If this was any indication of the kind of friends Lawrence had called upon, I could hardly wait to see the rest of them. Duff Henley was at least six foot four, and his solid frame radiated strength and energy. I'd have bet on him in a fight with any man, including Nash. He was a U.S. marshal.

"And this is my right-hand *man,* our photographer, Sidra Givens." Lawrence interrupted my thoughts with a grin.

Duff took my hand, but, unlike most large men, he held it gently. His eyes were the fearless blue I'd seen on other Western lawmen, and they took me in from head to foot.

"Pleased to meet you, ma'am."

"You eat yet, Duff?" Lawrence asked.

Duff laughed, a big, booming laugh that echoed around the lobby. "I was standin' there when they opened the door. Been ridin' all day and could 'a' downed a bear raw."

"I'd like to talk as soon as we can," Lawrence said. "Why not come in and have a cup of coffee with us, at least." Then he leaned closer. "We'll have to watch what we say in there, though. Spies all over the damn' place, and I'll tell you whose and why later."

"You don't have to," Duff replied. "I know what goes on in my territory."

He gave me his arm to escort me in to supper. "They have a good steak here," he said, eyes twinkling. "Last time I was in town it was only passable, but they must've got a new rustler."

We settled in his chairs and ordered almost immediately.

"Speaking of rustlers," Lawrence said, "they tell me that somebody took out Colonel Godbolt and said they were going to feed him something he'd never eaten before. He wanted to know what. The fellow said . . . 'Some of your own beef.' "

It was a story as old as the hills and it always had a different set of names to go with it, but it never failed to get a laugh. Duff was no different.

"If that happened, from what I know, he didn't think it was funny."

"He doesn't think anything's funny," I put in. "And around here, he's right."

Duff nodded. "So I hear. But there's a fellow upstairs you'll all want to meet as soon as possible. He ain't too used to ridin' and turned in early."

"Who?" Lawrence perked up, hoping, I thought, that his father had come through.

"Stan Gordon. U.S. Commissioner and Special Investigator for the Justice Department, right now, to boot. T.R. picked him personally after he got your wire."

Lawrence looked uncomfortable. He was always careful about revealing his connections with what he called "big bugs", thinking it might hurt in his dealings with many people.

Duff didn't notice Lawrence wince and went on. "Gordon looks like a nice mild fellow and is polite and considerate as all get out, but they tell me he's hell on wheels, especially if he gets on the case of crooks."

"He'll have a field day here." Lawrence gave him a grim smile. The food arrived. "When we're done, why don't we walk to where we're staying and we can talk. I rented a place. The walls here probably have ears."

When we had finished with our meal, Duff announced — "I'm ready if you folks are." — and pushed back his chair.

The two of them went on ahead, deep in earnest conversation. The last light was fading in the west, the sky that pale yellow that comes just before dark, and the mountains stood sharp and black against it.

For the first time in days I let myself relax. The marshal was here, and so far we'd not seen any of Godbolt's men lurking around. "Please keep Stefan and Jacky safe," I murmured, without knowing that my prayers were not to be answered and I could lay that at the door of Nash Fallon.

CHAPTER TWENTY-THREE

Happiness is a fleeting thing, as a rule, and mine lasted until we stepped out of the Oriental after breakfast the next morning.

Almost abreast of us was a small cavalcade consisting of Trig Cassidy, Nash Fallon, sporting a deputy sheriff's badge I'd never seen him wear before, and Stefan and Jacky with their hands tied to the horns of their saddles. Jacky was riding a grulla that I assumed was his beloved Poco, but he didn't look happy over the reunion.

When he saw us, his eyes lit with hope. "Ma!" he called, shrill as a bird. "Ma!"

I ran out into the street, dodging the wagons, burros, idlers that made up the early morning traffic.

Nash pulled up, and the rest stopped with him, and Lawrence came rapidly to my side. "What's this all about?" he demanded, eyeing Nash with something like ferocity.

"There's a warrant out for the kid."

"Was there a warrant out for the priest, too?"

"We're bringing him in for obstructing justice."

Lawrence snorted. "Justice? Fallon, do you have any idea what world you're living in? There won't be any justice here until your boss is dead or behind bars."

"I do my job," Nash said.

"Some job. I wouldn't have it on a gold platter. And you'd better see that nothing happens to either the priest or to Jacky. The U.S. marshal is in town, and so is the U.S. Commissioner, and they aren't on a holiday."

At that point Duff Henley joined us, but said nothing, simply looked Fallon over. For a moment I thought I saw surprise on his face, and looked quickly at Nash, but he was his usual stoic self.

"I like the kid," Nash said. "He's a fighter. Come to think of it, so is the *padre*. Nothing's gonna happen to either one of 'em while I'm around."

I looked at Stefan who hadn't said a word. "I took Jacky to our hide-out," he began. "He didn't stay hid. Fallon, here, brought his horse in as bait and staked it out in the cañon where Jacky could see it. Can you blame the boy?" To Fallon he said: "You

224

don't happen to have second sight, do you?"

Fallon said: "Common sense. I've been in this business a long while."

I expected Nash to try to stop Stefan's recitation, but he didn't. "Jacky went out to his horse. And then this . . . this devil's henchman grabbed him. When I came to help, they overpowered me."

From the bruises on his face, I judged that he had fought hard. One of his eyes was black, and there was a cut over the other.

And Nash had done this — had beaten up a priest, the man I loved — or had, at least, stood by and watched it done.

"You son-of-a-bitch," I said to him, and was pleased to see that for once he looked ashamed. "We'll get you out on bail," I said to Stefan.

Trig spoke for the first time. "I wouldn't bet on it. Not with old 'thirty years, next case' Crandall as judge. I've seen him sentence a guy to hang without a trial. When the guy's lawyer squawked, he threatened to hang him, too."

"What happened?" I asked, horrified at the state of affairs that had gone on, as I saw it, far too long.

"Turned out he didn't hang either one of 'em, but it took a troop of cavalry from Fort

225

Stanton to bail 'em out for a change of venue."

Jacky had been listening to all of this, slumped on his horse and miserable. "Are they gonna hang me?" he asked dolefully.

Not if this gunslinger has to break you out, was my instant but silent reply.

Lawrence laid a hand on Jacky's knee. There was, I noticed, a hole in his pants, probably a result of the fight. "We finally got some law here in Lost River. Don't worry. Nobody's going to hang you. Or Father Stefan, either," he added.

"And we can't stand here all day in the street," Nash said. "Let's get going."

I watched them all the way to the courthouse where I knew they'd be put behind bars. *So much for prayers.*

The small man who'd been watching from the steps of the hotel walked up to us. "What was that all about?" he asked Duff.

Duff told him.

At that point I guessed that this was Stan Gordon, the U.S. Commissioner, and my guess was proved right when he said: "Pity I was a little late. I could have convened court and taken them as federal prisoners. Any objections from the others, I'd have jugged them for contempt of court."

I couldn't contain my smile of approval.

Here was another of the kind we needed. When Duff introduced us, I approved even more of his good manners. He removed his hat like a true gentleman and bowed low over my hand. "My pleasure, ma'am," he said.

"And mine, sir," I said, and then got right to the point. "We need to find a lawyer, but there isn't one in this town that isn't afraid to take the case."

Behind his glasses, Gordon's eyes lit up. "As it happens, I'm licensed to practice in the territory. An old friend thought that might be necessary and took care of it before I left Washington."

Old friend! I thought. *I bet I know just who that old friend is, and thank God for him, Lawrence, and Lawrence, Senior! Maybe now we can get something done right around here!*

But there was also the question of bail money — which I certainly couldn't come up with. When I mentioned it, Lawrence intervened.

"I think I can manage it. *Pater* increased my allowance just before I came out here." He said it with a completely straight face, but his mouth was twitching.

This was the other side of Lawrence, the side he very rarely showed but which went a long way toward making him the likeable

227

man that he was. If he wasn't wealthy yet in his own right — and I was sure he was, and the remark about his father was just a joke — I'd bet his allowance had been raised to something like $50,000 a month. But Lawrence never mentioned his fortune, for which I gave him much credit. It was there, he accepted the fact, but he always expected to earn his own way through his own hard work.

"What do we do now?" I asked.

Stan Gordon said: "I, for one, get breakfast. I guess you've had yours, but I'd like you to join me so we can get acquainted."

Our crew had finished their breakfast and come out just in time to catch the tail end of our confrontation with Nash and his prisoners. Lawrence sent them down to our new quarters to begin getting specimens ready for me to photograph, then came inside with the rest.

At the breakfast table I made my first thorough inspection of U.S. Commissioner and Special Agent Stan Gordon. I liked what I saw. He could have been mistaken for a cigar drummer, but that was before one noticed his shrewd eyes and determined chin, that and the fact that those eyes didn't miss a thing.

His first words reassured me even more.

"Just so you know, I understand that the governor may be in Godbolt's pocket. That would be a great worry except that I'm authorized to have him replaced if the circumstances warrant. Now tell me what you know about Godbolt."

After a look around the room, Lawrence did. Gordon nodded occasionally, but didn't even ask a question, being too busy with ham and eggs, pancakes, fried potatoes, bread and butter, and several cups of coffee. How could such a small man, slender and with no paunch at all, have such an appetite?

When he finished, he wiped his mouth, then folded his napkin into a precise square before he spoke. "My first move is going to be to have Godbolt come in here. I intend to subpoena him as my first witness."

"He won't like it," Lawrence said. "May refuse to come."

Gordon's honest brown eyes turned to steel. "Let him," was all he said.

Duff Henley was tough, and Stan Gordon was no fool, but to take on Godbolt and his crew was going to take a good many deputies. Where were they coming from? I doubted that anyone in town wanted to take the job.

Lawrence looked pleased at Gordon's

229

obvious determination and with the fact that we at least had two good men on our side. He never, however, forgot his original purpose in coming to the valley and didn't do so now, but turned to me. "Would you mind going down and getting set up for pictures? We'll need a lot, and, as soon as you've finished, we can start packing."

I hated to miss out on any strategy sessions, but knew I'd intruded enough in what was normally and exclusively a male domain.

I needn't have worried. A few hours later, at lunch, Stan Gordon offered me a job that was to give me a ringside seat at the storm gathering around us.

"I want to have pictures of all the witnesses I call," he said. "For my records. Lawrence has kindly agreed to me hiring you for the job, if you want it."

I almost shouted: *Want it? I'd love it!*

"You can sit in and take notes, too. I'd be obliged if you did. The pay's double for that."

What was it I'd said about money only the day before? Once I'd finished here, I'd surely have enough to support myself and Jacky. Unless, of course, our maneuvering and strategies failed. But they wouldn't. Couldn't. I wasn't about to let that happen.

This was like offering a kid candy. I was going to get more candy than expected — a ringside seat at the final tragic rounds of the Godbolt reign on Lost River.

CHAPTER TWENTY-FOUR

Gordon didn't waste time slipping me into his organization. "I wonder if I can borrow Sidra for a couple of hours to get my office set up," he asked Lawrence, then grinned, acknowledging that his question was really a polite command. "The county doesn't know it yet, but I intend to take over the courtroom."

"And if they object?"

"They won't. Not when they find out what sort of change Uncle Theodore authorized me to pay for the proper quarters to uphold the majesty of the United States. I got my final instructions from him personally. He said . . . 'Show those fellows that the statute runs even out there among the horn toads.'"

I wondered if Gordon really was Roosevelt's nephew, or if that was only his wry method of referring to the President. But he didn't give me time to ask.

"Why don't all of you come down and

watch the fun while I rent my new office?" he said.

It was an invitation none of us could refuse.

We found Sheriff Briscoe in his office, which was fortunate, since he was the county's chief officer of the court when the district judge wasn't in town. Even the clerk of the court had to take orders from him.

Gordon didn't waste time laying out his proposition. Briscoe looked a little disconcerted and began his habitual tugging on his mustache. Obviously he'd already received orders to take the necessary steps with his new prisoners, and I knew very well what those orders entailed. Godbolt subscribed to the old Mexican saying: *los muertos no hablán* — the dead do not speak. It was a chilling thought that the only living witnesses to his evil doings were Jacky and me.

Briscoe's problem, of course, was that Stan Gordon's presence would impede the carrying out of Godbolt's orders, since the jail was in the courthouse. With a final tug, he said: "I'm sorry, Commissioner, but I can't be sure we won't want the court for our own judges in the next few days. Our J.P.s all use it when court ain't in session, and Judge Crandall is the probate judge and he uses it almost every day for something."

"We can vacate whenever they need the place and use your office here." Stan didn't change expression, but Briscoe had trouble getting his next words out.

"I'd like to help you, but the answer is no."

For the second time that day I saw Gordon's eyes turn to steel. "In that case, Sheriff, I guess I'll have to show you my letter of instructions from the President. It authorizes me to remove any territorial officers that in my opinion are attempting to obstruct justice, up to and including the governor."

He handed the letter to Briscoe, who read slowly through it, moving his lips as he labored with the big words. After he finished, he looked at Gordon, his shoulders slumped in defeat.

"It's my opinion that you're attempting to obstruct justice," Gordon said. "If you should have a sudden change of heart, I'd take that into consideration."

Briscoe was far from a fool. He knew when he was licked. All he said was: "OK. I've thought it over. There's no reason why you can't use the courtroom."

I could see the wheels turning in his head, and knew he'd go running to Godbolt the first chance he got. But at least they'd have to postpone whatever plans they had for Stefan and Jacky.

Gordon smiled amiably at Briscoe. "I thought you'd be reasonable."

Our first order of business was to fill out a subpoena for Godbolt, and Gordon had me look over his shoulder while he explained how to fill in each blank. "You'll be making out a lot of these for me," he said with a chuckle, then handed the completed paper over to Duff. "I'm sure the sheriff will provide you with a deputy if you need any help serving this. Maybe Nash Fallon."

"I'll go alone," Duff said, ignoring the joke. "I know the old bastard, pardon my French, Sidra. I doubt he'll give me any trouble."

I wasn't so sure of that. The way I saw it, Godbolt would give St. Peter trouble when he heard his final verdict.

"Don't you think the marshal is a little optimistic?" I asked Gordon when Duff had left.

"Maybe," he said. "We'll see. In the meantime, if you want to go down and help Lawrence, I won't be needing you for a while. If I do, I'll send someone for you."

I had what amounted to a photography studio set up downstairs in the old mill. The boys had made me a plank table, and we'd discovered a side room that served as a darkroom.

For the first time in days I felt reasonably happy and hummed softly to myself as I shot roll after roll of film of our various finds. I heard someone come in and stand, watching me, but I didn't turn around, thinking it was Dan or Hugh, or perhaps just a curious visitor, since everyone liked to watch photographers work.

When I did, I almost dropped my camera. Old Juan took off his hat and bowed to me, but the look in his eyes told me this wasn't a social call. He wasted no time coming to the point.

"The boy is in great danger. They will kill the *padre,* too." He spoke in a whisper and seemed to be watching the shadows in the corners of the room, searching for intruders.

I put down the camera and moved close to him. "What do you know? Tell me!"

His dark eyes reflected his urgency, but he wasn't entirely coherent due both to his difficulties with English and the fact that I was a woman, and an unknown quantity. I thought that perhaps the servant girl had told him I was trustworthy, or perhaps he'd simply decided for himself, after seeing me at the funeral. There was, however, more to it than that.

"The boy did not do it," he said. "But *el diablo* thinks he did. The boy knows too much about the killing of his father and mother. *El diablo*, he give me a message to give to the sheriff, but it is wrong, *señora*, believe me."

As well as I knew my name, I knew what was in that message. "When will they do it?" I asked. "How much time is there?"

He shrugged. "This I don't know. But soon, I think."

"Why did you come to me?"

"Because the old crow said I could trust you. She said you love the boy." His eyes pleaded with me to believe him.

I did. Completely. But the old crow? I searched my mind for an answer to that, then asked: "Who do you mean?"

He smiled for the first time. "The one you call Mercy."

At first I was stunned, then thought: *Why not? Mercy and all the homesteaders hated Godbolt, and Jacky was one of theirs. The Mexicans hated Godbolt. Why not an alliance? Why not the weak against the strong? It wouldn't have been the first time in history that such an unlikely army succeeded.*

"We have a plan, *señora*," he went on.

236

"With your help."

"Of course, I'll help. Tell me what I can do."

I listened and agreed, then saw Juan to the door. It was bold but possible. "I'll do my best," I assured him. "And I thank you for coming to me. Until tonight."

He bowed again. "God willing." And then he was gone, slipping out and away like a shadow.

In my room I washed face and hands and primped a little, priest or not, endangered or not, Stefan was the man I loved. To go to him with smudged cheeks and hair disheveled was unthinkable. There was another, more wicked reason. Several times I'd seen Briscoe looking me over with what seemed to be admiration. If I had to sweet-talk my way into the jail, I'd do it at my best.

With that, I put on my bonnet — old but still attractive, with its new ribbons — picked up my purse containing my trusty .41, and set off down the street.

It was hot and sultry, the beginning of the summer rainy season. To the south, a thundercloud was growing, brilliant white, edged in black and vivid against a turquoise sky. If it rained, would that help or hinder our plan?

As expected, Briscoe gave me no trouble

about visiting his prisoners, possibly because of the way I shamelessly batted my eyes, or because of the fact that Stan Gordon was in the nearby courtroom. Briscoe made a great show of rattling keys, holding doors for me, announcing my arrival in what he must have hoped was a cheerful voice.

"Ma? Is it you?" I heard Jacky before I saw him, small, expectant, peering through the bars.

Stefan stood behind him, and my heart turned over at the sight of his untended bruises, and the dingy cell with its two cots and chamber pot. To hide my feelings — and to be rid of him — I turned on Briscoe.

"You get me something to tend those cuts!" I demanded. "And you do it now!"

"But . . . I ain't supposed. . . ."

I stamped my foot and stuck my face close to his. "You heard me. Or do I have to call the Commissioner?"

He raised a hand to ward me off. "No. No, ma'am. I'll see to it."

"I'll be right here," I said, and made sure he was out of hearing before I turned to the bedraggled pair.

"Listen," I whispered. "We don't have much time."

As they heard me out, their eyes widened.

238

Stefan reached his hand through the bars and took mine. "Keep yourself safe, Sidra. We'll be all right."

"Yes," I said. "You will. So will I."

He pulled me closer, looked deep into my eyes. "Did you mean it? What you told me when you left?"

I love you. I mouthed the words, hesitating to speak them aloud.

If ever a man's heart showed in his eyes, it was then — in that horrible place where the sun couldn't penetrate, and where death lurked somewhere just out of sight.

"God be with us," he murmured.

The moment was shattered by Briscoe's return. He carried a basin, a cloth, and a bottle of what looked like iodine. I sighed, wishing for the herbs Lizzie Roanhorse had given me, then cheered myself with the thought that if all went well I would be able to use them later.

While Briscoe watched, I bathed Stefan's face, my fingers moving gently over the bruises, over the stubble of beard on his chin, and silently I cursed them all — Godbolt, Fallon, this two-bit sheriff with his ragged mustache watching me.

When I finished, I plastered a smile on my face for Briscoe's benefit, kissed Jacky, touched Stefan's arm. Then I almost ran —

out of the jail and back to the familiarity of my workshop.

Duff returned late that afternoon, and he had a sour-faced Godbolt with him. I hoped his presence wouldn't hinder our plan, since he was staying at his house at the edge of town, and, no doubt, would have some of his riders with him.

Gordon greeted him with his usual smoothness. "It was good of you to come in, Colonel. I'd like to talk to you before anyone else tomorrow."

"Anything to support Uncle Sam," Godbolt said as pleasantly as he could under the circumstances.

I was unable to eat much at supper and went to my room early, pleading a headache and so keyed up I could barely keep from fidgeting and arousing Lawrence's concern. It would be just like him to want to keep me company, and I doubted he'd agree to my abetting a suspected murderer in a jail break. Once in my room, I lay awake, waiting, a candle lit so I could watch the clock.

"The beer wagon, it goes down the alley behind the jail every night," Juan had told me. "Tonight we will help to drive it."

At half past ten I put on my dark cloak, picked up my bag with my .41 inside and added a Colt for Stefan, and then crept down the stairs. Juan had been correct in one thing. The alley was dark and deserted except for a prowling cat that slipped past me and disappeared into the shadows. What little light there was came from the stars and a sliver of new moon already far to the west. The rain had passed us by. The sky was cloudless.

I waited, digging my fingernails into sweaty palms, my heart beating so hard I nearly choked. Then I saw the wagon, pulled by two large draft horses, coming slowly toward me.

Juan's voice came out of the dark. "We will wait until we hear the shooting." Then he gave me a hand and pulled me up beside him on the seat.

I knew Fallon was on guard at the jail — Fallon who'd promised to keep Jacky safe, but would he keep that promise in an actual showdown? Could I really trust a killer who had been Godbolt's right arm and had terrorized the valley? And could I shoot him, the man who'd aroused my passion, even to protect the man I loved? So many questions. So few answers. Like everything else in my life, I'd have to live through it to find out.

When the shooting started, it ripped the night like a knife. From the end of Main

Street came the dancing light of a fire, and we could hear shouting as people ran out of their houses and the saloons emptied. Still the gunshots continued. I was almost certain I heard the sound of Mercy's scatter-gun.

"*¡Andale!*" Juan shook the reins, and the wagon lurched forward.

There was shouting in front of the jail, but the alley remained deserted. Juan and the other man, whose face I never saw, leaped down, unhitched the traces, and re-hooked them to the chain that had been fastened to the bars of the window. Then the big horses leaned into their collars, and, with a sound like rusty nails being pulled, the bars came loose.

Jacky crawled through first, then Stefan followed, landing nimbly on the ground. From somewhere inside, we heard a voice yelling: "Hey! Stop there!" I handed Stefan his six-shooter, hitched up my skirts, and ran up the alley a short way, then ducked between two buildings. We stopped under a clump of cottonwoods and checked our back trail.

I wasn't sure, but I thought I saw a shadowy figure highlighted against the glare of the fire at the end of the street.

"Fallon!" Jacky said, and I felt the tension in him.

"We can't stay here. If he comes, we'll have to shoot him." Stefan groped for my hand in the dark.

"We're going back to the mill as soon as I catch my breath," I told them. "And, yes, we'll shoot if we have to."

We stood for a minute, watching, waiting, but if it was Nash, he disappeared, for which I uttered one of those prayers that lately seemed to come so easily to my lips.

Cautiously we made our way back down the alley to the mill where we found Lawrence and the crew in a state of agitation with all lanterns lit.

"What the hell is going on here?" Lawrence demanded in his most imperious voice.

"That should be obvious," I said. "Put those damned lanterns out. Somebody's probably watching the place."

He scanned our faces, and I realized that he was trying not to laugh.

"What's funny?" I demanded.

"There are times, Sidra Givens, when you amaze me," he said. "And then there are times when I should take you over my knee and spank you." To Hugh and Dan, he said: "Stay here. Lock the door and don't let anybody in. Scott, keep your eye on the corral. Stefan and Jacky . . . upstairs. Now!"

"I'm hungry," Jacky said.

Spoken like a true survivor! I let out a sigh of relief, and Stefan said: "The food in the jail wasn't anything like yours, Sidra."

Only after I'd brought them some bread and cheese and a bowl of ripe peaches did the reaction set in. I began to shake from head to foot, imagining what could have happened.

Even in the dark, Stefan sensed my state, and put his arms around me. "Hush," he said. "You are the bravest woman I know. I owe you my life."

He was warm and comforting. My body fit into his as if we were two pieces of a puzzle. I would have stayed where I was indefinitely, except that Jacky was watching.

"I didn't know priests were allowed to do that," he said through a mouthful.

"This priest is." Stefan released me and stood up. "And this woman . . . and you and I . . . are going to bed. We have all had a very busy night."

CHAPTER TWENTY-FIVE

Mercy's nesters had burned Godbolt's town house to the ground. He spent the night at the hotel, clad only in his nightshirt, but none of this deterred Stan Gordon from proceeding with his deposition hearings. He merely postponed them for a few hours.

When Godbolt arrived, it was 10 a.m., and he looked exactly like what he was — a man whose world had been turned upside down, all in a few days. His skin was ashen, his hands trembled, and he walked with the unsteady gait of an old man. I almost pitied him, until he began to bluster and it became obvious that, inside, he was the same wily manipulator.

"You see what this place is like!" he said to Commissioner Gordon. "Nothing is safe. Those nesters tried to burn my ranch, killed my daughter, and the little mudsill who did it was broken out of jail last night. My town house is destroyed, and whoever did it took my safe. I had five thousand dollars in double eagles in it!"

Score one for the old crow! I thought. *With that much money, her army had enough to hire their own gunmen, to feed and clothe themselves, and take care of their own. Well done, Mercy!*

"Was anyone killed?" Gordon asked.

Godbolt looked surprised. He hadn't thought to find out since he himself was still intact. "I don't know."

Gordon's face showed what he thought of that. "I understand that when people around

245

here get burned out, they're usually murdered in the bargain."

Godbolt drew himself up. "The riff-raff are fighting with each other and trying to ruin and implicate me. I hope you get to the bottom of all this."

"That's why I'm here," Gordon said. He swore Godbolt in, then started his questioning.

"Colonel Godbolt, what can you tell me in your own words about the violence in this part of the country and what you think is behind it."

Godbolt thought that over for a while before speaking. He seemed a different man from the arrogant rancher who'd driven up to our camp, and the new clothes he'd gotten hung from his skinny body as if from a scarecrow. When he did begin to speak, his voice was weak and rusty as if his throat was dry. I wondered if he was, in fact, apprehensive at having to face a man who could destroy his fiefdom.

"Three years ago the government unwisely opened the Lost River Valley to homesteaders under the Desert Homestead Act." He cleared his throat, then went on. "It allows a six hundred and forty acre claim, bigger than the one hundred and sixty that ruined the cattle country back east. But six hundred and forty acres won't raise more than ten cows in the dry years we have here. It was foolish of these people to think they could go into the cattle business. When they found out they couldn't make it, those along the river turned to farming and hay raising. The problem was that the Mexicans who'd always farmed there already occupied all the good land. That's what led to the violence we've had recently." He paused to see how that was being taken.

"Don't the homesteaders use the open range just as you do to raise cows?" Gordon asked. "Could even you make it with your big outfit without the open range?"

Godbolt looked uncomfortable. "It's the custom of the country that cattlemen are allowed to use government land until it's filed on. There must be a million acres still out there. I use my share of it."

"And what do you consider your share of it?"

"It's hard to say. Most of us, up till recently, got along fine without any problem."

Deftly Gordon changed the subject. "You say the trouble started three years ago. Isn't that when you yourself came into this country and started ranching?"

Godbolt's eyes narrowed — the snake

again. "Are you accusing me of starting all the trouble here? I've been the target of rustling and burning and having my cowboys shot. A half dozen of them were murdered just a couple days ago. I've ordered the rest to go armed from now on."

How practiced he was at lying! I noticed that as he went on, he gained confidence, as if he'd convinced himself of the truth of what he was saying. Maybe he had. The thought occurred to me that he was on the ragged edge and might go over the brink if pushed.

"I presume the sheriff is investigating these murders," Gordon said. "But it's odd he didn't mention them to me before now. How did they come about and what makes you call them murders?"

Godbolt took a deep breath, giving himself time to think about a question he obviously hadn't expected, one to which he realized an answer would have to be forthcoming to sound convincing.

"In this case it goes back a ways, and I'll have to give you the background." At Gordon's nod, he went on. "An old hardcase from Missouri, Harve Fellows and his wife Mercy came into the valley dead broke with a couple of kids to feed. Out of the goodness of her heart an old lady, Granny

Prosser, gave them jobs on her ranch. They homesteaded for themselves but still worked for her, and I understand rustled her cows to set up their own herd. Then they decided to get rid of her and steal her range. Harve poisoned her. Another old Missouri murderer named Arnason was in it with them. My foreman, Nash Fallon, came along just before she died, and tried to help her. She told him that Fellows had poisoned her. But Fellows and Arnason tried to hang the poisoning on Fallon. It didn't work, though. Sheriff Briscoe investigated and found a bottle of the poison in a shed at Fellows's ranch. A jury convicted him, and we hung him just last month."

He sounded so convincing that even I was ready to believe him, especially since I found it hard to believe that Fallon would poison an old woman's tea. However, knowing Godbolt's ways, I was sure that the poison had been planted in Harve's shed, regardless of who had administered it.

Gordon said nothing, simply looked at Godbolt. The colonel went on. "Fellows's widow apparently had a falling out with the Arnasons and they burned her out."

Gordon interrupted: "Before you go on, I understand that you have taken over Granny Prosser's ranch. How did that come about?"

Godbolt looked pleased with his ready answer to that one. "I loaned her money to keep her going. I held the mortgage and foreclosed."

"I assume this is all on record."

"Of course," he said. "I do everything legal and proper."

Gordon was noncommittal, but gestured for Godbolt to continue.

"It looks to me like Mercy Fellows has lost her mind, not that she had much of one to begin with. She's been camping out with her kids and threatening anyone who comes near with a shotgun. I was told she was butchering her neighbors' beef, so I sent some of my cowboys to see if any of my cattle were up her way. They didn't come back, and the sheriff sent some deputies to see what happened. They haven't come back yet, either."

You almost got that right, I thought, *but my how you can twist facts in your favor.*

"How long ago was that?"

"A couple of days."

"It seems to me that by now the sheriff would have taken a posse up there to investigate."

"He did."

"And?"

"So far he hasn't found a single body."

250

Gordon raised his eyebrows. "That's hard to believe. Bodies don't disappear."

"Yes, well. . . ." Godbolt cleared his throat. "There have been rumors for months that there's something called the dead wagon that goes around the country disposing of evidence of murders in some private burial ground. The sheriff found wagon tracks and followed them, but they didn't lead anywhere, or at least not to a grave. What he found was old Mercy Fellows and a gang that's thrown in with her. They're in the cañon, forted up. They drove off my . . ." — he caught himself — "the sheriff's posse."

"You're telling me the sheriff is unable to enforce the law here?" Gordon asked.

"You have to understand the nature of these people." Godbolt was condescending, a mistake, I thought. "Like common criminals, they have little or no respect for the law. So little that Briscoe is thinking of going to the governor."

Gordon hid a smile. "No need for that, Colonel. I came here because Doctor Haslett wired to Washington, through influential friends, and suggested that the federal government investigate the problem."

"Haslett simply beat us to it," Godbolt said quickly. "You know that a sheriff hesitates to admit he can't enforce the law.

251

Do you blame Briscoe?"

"Do you?" Gordon leaned across the table and came in for the kill. "I understand your daughter was murdered. Yet neither you nor he did anything about it."

"I. . . ." He broke off, his grief obvious.

"I'm sorry," Gordon said. "But it's a fact, isn't it?"

"Yes," Godbolt said with an obvious effort. Then he collapsed onto the table sobbing. "Celine, Celine, my little girl."

If it was an act, it was a good one. In spite of what I knew, I pitied him.

Gordon realized further questions were useless, and motioned to Duff. "We'll call him back later, if we need him. Let's bring in someone else."

Godbolt left the courtroom. I hadn't taken his photo as Gordon had wanted me to do with each witness. I had reason to regret it all too soon.

After Duff had escorted Godbolt out, Gordon looked at me. "What do you think?"

"A very clever liar. He used just enough of the truth to make it sound convincing. As they'd say back in Connecticut, 'he lies like a rug'."

"Bring in the next witness," Gordon said with a shake of his head.

Both Lawrence and I, knowing as much

as anyone of the whole picture, had given Gordon the names of those he should cross-examine. Our next witness was Roberto Rodriguez.

I had never seen Roberto before and immediately understood his reputation as a ladies' man. He was as handsome as Nash but Latin, with classical features and smoldering dark eyes that, I supposed, would have given many a woman palpitations. He came in with a proud strut, concealing his nervousness with bravado.

He shifted uncomfortably in his chair as Gordon swore him in. Perhaps, I thought, he was apprehensive about being questioned by an emissary of the President of the United States. To him, Stan Gordon must have appeared like the king's regent.

Gordon was either fantastically lucky or the shrewdest interrogator I had ever seen, because his first question was the only one he needed.

"I understand, Roberto, that you were one of the last people to see María Gonzalez alive."

I assumed that by "alive" he meant when María had been escorted to the train.

Roberto jumped to an entirely different assumption.

"I didn't kill her! I loved her! We were sup-

253

posed to run away together. It was why I was there. The only reason. That bitch!"

Gordon was as startled as I was, but he concealed it remarkably well. "Where were you when she was killed? And what bitch are you talking about?"

Roberto's handsome face twisted with what looked like contempt. Or perhaps it was hatred. "Celine, *señor.* She was a bad woman. Very bad. You understand? And we were on the road to Lost River by the short cut from Hatch's Siding when it happened."

Gordon had a mind like a finely oiled machine. He hadn't forgotten a thing about the briefings Lawrence and I had provided him. "That's why you hid the bodies in the caves, right?"

I thought — *God how quick and shrewd he is!* — and noted the look of admiration for what Gordon was doing on Duff's face, too.

Roberto wiped his face on his sleeve and went on. "We left the train at Hatch's Siding. Celine had a surrey and *mucho dinero* that she said she would give us if we left and never came back. María and I . . . we loved each other, *señor.* You must believe it. But she was afraid of *el diablo.* . . . of what he would do to her. And there was the child. He loved that boy, maybe more than anyone, and he told María he would always take care

254

of them."

It was easy to understand María's revulsion. Godbolt was not only evil but one of the most unattractive men I'd ever seen. But she had been caught in a web of deceit and necessity — a web, I saw now, that Celine had spun to be rid of her rivals for her inheritance.

"And you camped by the caves for the night, right?" Gordon prompted.

Roberto looked as though he thought the Commissioner could read his mind.

"*Sí*. And in the morning María was still afraid to leave because of the boy. The colonel loved him, and she think it would not be right to run away. We wanted to, *señor*. We were lovers, and many times she told me she got sick when *el diablo* touched her. I had thought to kill him!

"Then Celine, she got real mad, and scream at us, and the boy. He was scared and ran away. He. . . ." Roberto closed his eyes for a moment, as if he was reliving the awful scene. "He . . . fell over the cliff, and María ran after him. I think he was already dead. His neck broken. María looked over the edge and screamed. And then Celine . . . maybe she had not planned to kill María, but the devil whispered to her. She pushed María over. I saw her, *señor,* with my own eyes. When I climb down, they were both dead."

Sobbing, he stopped, and who could blame him? Not I. Not Stan Gordon. "I loved her!" he said again. "And I loved the boy, even if he was not mine. I wish I had died with them. Instead, I help to put them in the cave. Celine, she promised me *mucho dinero,* as long as I live, to say nothing, but that promise, it burns inside me like a sickness." With that he buried his face in his hands.

Gordon gave him time to pull himself together, then got up and put a hand on his shoulder. "I'm sorry," he said in a low voice. "And I do believe you."

Roberto looked up at him with tears on his face. "*Gracias, Señor* Commissioner. I would not lie about a thing like this." He looked first at me, then at Duff to see if we also believed him.

Duff said: "It makes sense to me."

I said nothing, but wished I could go over and hug the poor man. So much senseless misery! So much greed and power madness! And all to be laid at Godbolt's door. And at his daughter's who, at the last, had proved to be cast in her father's image.

Gordon said to Roberto: "That's all I have to ask you now. I may call you back later.

Don't leave town and tell absolutely no one what you have said here."

Roberto crossed himself and said: "*Sí, señor*. I promise in the name of God."

Hugh Stiles, arriving out of breath, almost ran into Roberto. "Godbolt has a big bunch of his killers all over town!" he said. "There must be fifty of them. And we think they know Jacky and the *padre* are at our place."

Duff looked across at Gordon. "I'd better get over there."

Gordon said: "If Godbolt is still with us, handcuff him to the bars on a cell. If you put him in one, his buddy the sheriff will let him out."

"He is out," Hugh said. "He's down there in that damn' surrey of his and has about ten of his men with him right across the street from our place."

Duff headed for the door. "I'll handle it."

"I'm coming with you," Gordon said.

We all left together, me conscious of my comforting equalizer in its usual place.

CHAPTER TWENTY-SIX

I give our boys high marks for grit. They weren't gunmen, but they all were out behind the front wall, holding rifles ready, eyeing Godbolt and his crew. Apparently

257

the colonel hadn't yet made up his mind just what he wanted to do, but I was sure he wanted Jacky dead, and Stefan along with him. Then I'd be the last witness left alive.

One shot! I thought. *One. And we'd be safe.* What prevented me? I'll never know.

Godbolt sat in his surrey looking like a mad man, one with nothing to lose from a mass killing. He could run for Mexico, and the U.S. would never get him extradited in view of conditions there. In Mexico he'd live like a king as he had before, probably thinking his young mistress and son would be with him at his beck and call.

Duff headed straight up the street for Godbolt, with Lawrence and Gordon in step beside him. I followed at their heels, attempting to make myself inconspicuous. It would be just like Lawrence to order me to go back for my safety.

Gordon, as the ranking official, stopped beside the surrey and said to Godbolt: "I'm ready to go on with the hearing."

"Well, I'm not." The words shot out like bullets, accompanied by a spray of spittle, and it was at that point that his men began shifting their horses so they wouldn't be bunched up if shooting started.

Duff stepped up beside Gordon. "Colonel,

there's no sense in starting trouble we can avoid. No one has accused you of anything, and there's no evidence that you've done anything that can be proven. Mister Gordon simply wants to get the record straight."

"Well, he can go to hell!" Godbolt's hands were twitching.

I thought he really was balanced on the edge and evidently Duff did, too. When he spoke again, he was still unruffled, but he had his hand on his pistol butt. "You know," he said, "if Mister Gordon gives the word, I'll have to try and take you in. Your men will get me, but I'll get you."

Before Godbolt could answer, Nash Fallon rode up and diverted everyone's attention. He stopped beside the surrey, placing his horse between it, Duff, and our party. I had had my eyes on the middle button of Godbolt's vest with the full intention of "increasing my bag", as Mercy would put it, but now Nash shielded his boss.

He leaned down and said something we couldn't hear, but Godbolt's expression changed to astonishment — or was it panic?

A minute later I learned the reason when a squad of U.S. Negro cavalrymen — six and a sergeant — came toward us at a fast trot.

"Our posse finally got here. I wonder what

took them so long," Duff said to Stan Gordon.

I didn't care why they were late so long as they were here. I hadn't even known they were on the way, but I was certainly glad to see them. Even the most hardened criminals hesitated to fire on U.S. troops, and this was as neat a squad of soldiers as I had ever seen.

All of Godbolt's earlier bluster had disappeared. He stared at the soldiers as if he couldn't believe his eyes, and, when Duff said to him — "How are the odds shaping up now, Colonel?" — he actually laughed. Or at least that's what the harsh noise sounded like.

Godbolt was a gambler, but not a fool, and not quite ready to die. To Stan Gordon he said: "I guess I'm ready to complete our little interview, if that's what you want to call it." Then he turned his team and started toward the courthouse. Over his shoulder, loud enough to be heard by everyone, he said to Fallon: "Keep our men in town."

Gordon led the way back up the street. Duff followed, after asking the sergeant to come along and mount a guard on the premises.

Once back inside, Gordon wasted no time reopening his court, saying to Godbolt:

"Consider yourself still sworn." His first question was right to the point. "What was the big idea of that affair down at Doctor Lawrence's building?"

Godbolt was as direct. "I have reason to believe that the young guttersnipe who murdered my daughter is being sheltered there."

Gordon shot back: "Two questions immediately occur to me, and they are, what gives you the idea that this particular 'guttersnipe', as you so delicately put it, killed your daughter, and what makes you think he's being sheltered by law abiding citizens?"

"The boy, Jacky Chastain, thinks I had my men kill his parents," Godbolt snarled. "But anyone with a lick of sense knows it was either that crazy woman and her nester crowd or the Mexicans. But that wouldn't cut any ice with the Chastain kid. He had the motive to kill Celine to get even with me, and he had the chance. He followed my daughter from Doctor Haslett's camp and did it. These people" — he gave me a withering glance — "this woman, were sheltering the boy in their camp even then."

"Wait a minute," Gordon interrupted, "and forget my first questions for now. Why did they need to shelter the boy, as you put

261

it? From what?"

"He tried to kill my foreman, Nash Fallon, who came along just after his parents were killed and their place was burned out. Nash was in the area and came on the run to help, but the kid thought he was with the killers. He took a couple of shots at Nash before he got away."

"I see. I suppose Mister Fallon will testify to this?"

Godbolt nodded, looking uncomfortable. He'd cooked up that story about Nash on the spur of the moment. Now what he needed was the opportunity to fill Nash in.

Obviously Gordon had the same thought, and turned to Duff. "Go and bring Fallon in if you can find him," he said, and then resumed with his interrogation.

"Let's get back to the second part of my question. What makes you think Doctor Haslett and Missus Givens are protecting Jacky Chastain now?"

"Because my people have been watching them. The boy and the priest went there right after someone broke them out of jail last night." He gave me a pointed stare.

"And why were you having law-abiding citizens watched?"

Before the colonel could answer, Duff came back in. "Fallon isn't around."

At that, Godbolt looked relieved. "When you find him, I'm sure he'll corroborate what I told you."

Yes, indeed, I thought. *Especially if you get to him first.*

Gordon, obviously, was thinking the same thing and decided to prevent the two from getting their stories straight. "Take Mister Godbolt into custody," he said to Duff.

"Now look here!" Godbolt pounded on the table with a clenched fist. "There's no reason for you to hold me. You yourself said nothing could be proved!"

"Just a precaution," Gordon said without changing expression. "I don't want you wandering off and getting into more trouble."

Duff started out with his prisoner just as Fallon was coming in. Godbolt, quick to take advantage of the situation, shoved Duff into the wall and ran past Nash, yelling to him: "Hold them off!"

Instinctively Nash jerked his pistol with a lightning move. "Everybody stand hitched!" he yelled. "What the hell is going on?"

"Take it easy, Nash," Duff said. "Your boss just got backed into a corner he isn't apt to get out of unless he wants to fight the U.S. government. I suspect he wants you and his men to take over the town while he runs for

263

Mexico."

Nash reholstered his pistol and surprised all of us. "I wouldn't put anything past the crazy old bastard. Let him run. Now someone told me y'all wanted to talk to me."

"True," Gordon said. "But first how about catching up to your boss and telling him that there are two companies of cavalry right behind that sergeant out there. He isn't running this country any more. *I* am. You can also tell him he's going to get full justice, but the only way he's going to hang onto his property is to comply with the law. And tell him we've uncovered some news he'll want to hear about María Gonzalez."

For once, Nash's surprise showed on his face. Plainly he didn't know she was dead, hadn't been anywhere near the site of the murders. Unnoticed, I let out a small sigh of relief.

As I'd found out, Stan Gordon was a master at thinking ahead. Nash was no sooner out the door than he turned to Duff. "Round up that fellow Roberto and put him in protective custody. Things are moving a little too fast, and I don't want them to get out of control. What I want is to have Roberto tell old Godbolt what he told us. Otherwise, the colonel will be trying for the rest of his life to get that boy Jacky killed."

264

Then Gordon turned to me. "Do you think Godbolt will believe Roberto? You think he'll believe his daughter was a murderess? I can see him accusing Roberto of killing both women."

Lawrence said: "Nothing he says or does . . . or thinks, for that matter . . . would surprise me."

It was only a few minutes later that Duff came back with Roberto, followed shortly by Fallon with the colonel. The tension in the room was so thick I could have photographed it, a ghostly image.

Gordon indicated the spectator section of the courtroom. "Please everyone take a seat here in the front row."

We did as we were told. Then the Commissioner dropped his bombshell.

"Colonel Godbolt, I don't want to distress you, but we have had testimony indicating that your . . . how should I put it? . . . *friend,* María Gonzalez, has been found dead."

I was watching Godbolt's face, and read total disbelief.

"No," he said. "I don't believe it. She's still at my ranch in Mexico. Who told you this lie? And why?"

"I'm not going to tell you just yet, but I am sure she was murdered near the camp of Doctor Haslett. Her body and that of a

265

small male child were found hidden in a cave near the murder site."

At first, the mention of the child seemed to have escaped him. He was still in a state of denial and looking around for a scapegoat. He picked Lawrence. "What do you have to say about this, if it's true?"

"I found the bodies," Lawrence told him. "But they'd been there for several weeks. Before we even came into Lost River Cañon."

Fallon was the next to come under Godbolt's anger. "I pay you to know everything that goes on in this country. Is it true?"

Nash shrugged, his face impassive. "I have no idea."

"You helped escort her out of the country. You and Roberto and Juan. Why would she come back? I can't believe any of this."

"Señor." Roberto couldn't contain himself any longer. "I know that it is true. I loved María years before you saw her and took her for your own. I still love her." He broke into unashamed tears.

Godbolt half rose from his chair and reached for his pistol. "You were her lover! Then you killed her! You were jealous!"

Duff clamped a hand on Godbolt's arm and took the gun from him.

Through his tears Roberto whimpered: "I

would never have killed her."

"Then how do you know she's dead? How do any of you know?"

Not caring that he'd already gone too far, Roberto blurted: "Because I saw her killed."

"You saw?" Godbolt was screaming, the veins standing out on his temples. "You saw and didn't stop it? But you sit there and say you loved her? You greaser Lothario, you don't know what love is! Now tell me who you saw kill her."

At Godbolt's racial slur, Robert's lips twisted into a sneer. All his hatred of this man they all called *el diablo* showed on his face. "Your bitch daughter killed her, *el diablo.* I couldn't move fast enough to stop her."

For a moment Godbolt was speechless. Then he asked: "Why didn't you tell me? Oh, I know why not. You were afraid to because you killed her yourself, just as I said! Celine would never have done such a thing. Not Celine. You're lying!"

Then, without warning, his mask crumbled. Behind it was the face of a ruined man. "I can't believe María's dead! And my boy. How can it be?" His expression changed again as another thought struck him. "You were sniffing around Celine, too. I knew it. She told me she'd have nothing

267

to do with a greaser. So what did you do? Kill her when she turned you down? It would be just like your kind." He turned to the Commissioner. "You'll have to prove to me that María is dead."

At that point, having heard enough, I stuck my nose in where perhaps it would have been better to remain silent, but I thought not. I certainly didn't foresee the consequences.

"I can prove she is dead, Mister Godbolt." I drew from my purse a stack of photos and handed him the one of the dead María with the medallion on her crossed hands. "We found this on her body and buried it with her. I think you may recognize it."

He stared at the photo a long while, barely breathing. "This can't be," he muttered. "She was . . . she was so beautiful. Like an angel. What did they do to her? I think I'm going to be sick."

Gordon gestured to Duff to escort Godbolt to the men's room. The old man was visibly shaken, stumbling as he got out of his chair and leaning heavily on Duff for support.

"Poor bastard," Lawrence said to no one in particular. "I almost feel sorry for him."

"Maybe I shouldn't have sprung that picture on him like that," I said, guilty after the fact.

Gordon peered at me over his glasses. "It had to be done sometime, Sidra. Maybe now we'll get the truth out of him."

The shot startled us all. For one second I wondered if Godbolt had shot Duff with a hide-out gun, and, with the others, I ran out into the hall.

Duff came out of the men's room, looking grim. "He had a Forty-One dinky in his pocket. He's in there . . . dead."

So the reign of terror came to an end in Lost River. It hadn't happened the way I had supposed it would, with a final, bloody showdown like that in Lincoln Country in 1878. And we had one man to thank for that — Stan Gordon. He'd made a gamble, played the cards he'd been dealt, sifted through the lies and deceit until he found the truth.

Stefan and Jacky were free. With Godbolt dead, no one would think to bring charges against the boy — or against Stefan for helping him. And Mercy and her followers now had a fair chance to wrest a living from that hard, unforgiving, but beautiful valley.

Who had killed Celine? The mystery was never solved. It could even have been Nash, although his actions belied that notion. That left Roberto, Mercy, and Juan — Juan who had come to me convinced of Jacky's innocence. Juan who had lost a daughter and a grandchild, and whose obsidian eyes gave nothing away.

I never saw Nash again, nor did I ever hear anyone else had. After Godbolt shot himself, while we were all too busy to notice, he rode out, the Black Knight of legend, on that big black horse of his, but he left a part of himself with me. Perhaps he took a part of me with him. I hope so.

EPILOGUE

The cottonwoods by the river were brilliant gold in the afternoon light, and the air had a bite to it like the tartness of an apple. I stood looking out and thinking how nothing remains the same, not the seasons, not life.

Everything was different now. I was no longer the penniless photographer who'd jumped at the chance to go to Lost River. I was Sidra Givens, a woman of consequence, whose photographs were on exhibit in Washington, who'd met the President and been charmed the way everyone was charmed by his manner, his knowledge, the twinkle in his eye.

And thanks to Stan Gordon, I was a mother at last. After the furor over Godbolt's death, he'd signed the adoption papers and made it official. He'd also registered the Chastain ranch in Jacky's name, saying: "It's his inheritance. It'll pay off."

That's when we found out about the seam of coal that lay under the valley, the unseen riches that had driven Godbolt mad and, in the end, cost him his life.

Jacky, of course, had gone with me to Washington and had become something of a hero to his schoolmates. He'd ridden cross-country on the train, toured the Capitol, actually shaken the President's hand, and then written an essay on his experience that was printed in the paper.

Now it appeared that I was mother to a budding journalist, one who spent every day after school in the newspaper office, asking questions and coming home smudged with ink.

We had both changed, and he, at least, was happy. Oh, so was I, for I'd gotten my wishes. Yet, on that day, I knew the magic ingredient that was necessary to complete the picture was missing.

I stepped outside, looked up at the sky that had turned the soft blue of autumn. A few leaves drifted down and landed on my face, light as a kiss. There was no lying to myself. The change in me was deeper than success. It had nothing to do with anything except my heart. And Stefan. Always I came back to him, to the days after Godbolt's suicide and our parting.

■ ■ ■ ■

Lawrence and the crew had gone, along with Stan Gordon, and Duff had ridden out early that morning. My wagon was packed and ready in the yard beside the mill, and beyond that, out in the street, the residents of Lost River were going about their business. I was not imagining the fact that they did so with a cheerfulness that had been lacking under Godbolt's reign. A man whistling somewhere, the laughter of women on their way to the market, the squeal of the woodcutter's burro, blended together — a musical collage that I ignored. On that day, all I knew was my own misery, an ache that weighed me down as if I was made of stone. Stefan was leaving — back to the mission. We had talked into the night but reached no conclusion, which, of course was typical.

I was angry at him and at myself. "So you've discovered you have a conscience," I'd said, accusing. "A little late for that, isn't it?"

The lamplight cast a halo around his head. He seemed a Byzantine icon, a saint struggling against the desires of the flesh, but, when he answered, he was firm.

"Until I can forgive myself, there will be no forgiveness. This is not about us, Sidra."

I laughed. "Yes it is. It's only about us. Mostly about you who can't make up your mind."

"Exactly." He got up, splintering the halo. What I saw then was a man in pain. "What I ask," he said slowly, "what I'll do with or without your understanding, is to come to terms with myself and my life. If your love turns to hate. . . ." He held out his hands, palms up. "I'll take that chance."

"I'll never hate you."

"Then watch the road for me. And pray." He left without a word, and with him the light in the room went out.

It had been more than a year. What hopes I had were gone. What remained were memories, an emptiness that even motherhood could not fill. I had done as Stefan asked — watched and prayed — but the road remained empty, and the prayers had worn out.

The mesas that bound the river were black in the slant of late afternoon sun. Against them the trees stood out, an eruption of gold. I went back inside, scribbled a note for Jacky, picked up my Kodak, and left the house. Color photography was still a dream, but light and dark could be caught with a click of the shutter — the two faces of earth — sun and shadow, laughter and tears.

I made my way down to the river that ran between the mesas like a spill of mercury, its end predestined by the tilt of the land, the shape of a continent, the oceans that waited for replenishment.

Like me, I thought. *Just like me,* and then focused on the reeds at the shore, the ripples of silver water and how they reflected sky.

How long I wandered there I cannot, now, say. I lost myself that afternoon in visions, in the remnants of my old passion for seeing. I lost myself, then sat down on the sand and let my mind run with the current.

"If you will lend me your camera, I would like to photograph you."

Stefan stood a few feet away. He was smiling, the brilliance of the river caught in his eyes.

"What . . . how?" I couldn't speak, couldn't for the life of me move for fear my illusion would vanish.

"You left a note. I followed." He came toward me, lifted me up, and I knew then that he was real.

"What took you so long?" I asked — a question that could have been construed as a challenge.

He slipped an arm around my waist. "Let's walk and I will explain. When I left you, I went out into the desert, and, as always, I talked to God. But I was asking questions only I could answer. Why had I done what I'd done, why had I taken my vows and then tossed them away at the first temptation?"

Worried, I looked up at him. "You mean I was the snake in the garden and not Eve?"

He chuckled. "No, my dear Sidra, that's not it. The temptation was life itself. The reality. The . . . how shall I say it? . . . the whole of it, and not just a part. I felt I had been living as a voyeur . . . watching, wanting, tasting existence through the feelings of others. Half a person, half a man, half a not-very-good priest. What you did, without knowing you were doing it, was wake me to the fact that I needed to be whole."

"And now?" I prompted, still dangling from the thinnest of threads.

"Don't rush me." He planted a kiss on my hair to soften his words. "I wandered in the desert and came to a place that seemed the end of the earth. Rocks, sand, dying trees. A horrible place. A wasteland. It reminded me of myself, and I didn't like what I saw. I was afraid, Sidra. Afraid of my own barrenness."

As always, I leaped to his defense. "You're not a wasteland! How can you compare yourself to . . . to that?"

"I can, and I did. And I took it as my answer. Back at the mission, I explained myself to my superior and asked to be released from my vows. Not a simple request, and something that doesn't happen overnight. But you see me here . . . a man yet to be born."

I went limp with relief, buried my face in my hands to hide my joy and tears. And then humor rescued me. I peeped at him through my fingers. "Are you asking me to be your mother?"

His laughter was a trumpet blast. It echoed off the mesas, mingled with the sound of water, and he spun me around to its music in a dance unrehearsed.

"No!" he said when his laughter subsided. "Not that. Will you be my mate, my wife, my conscience, and my friend, Sidra Givens?"

There was only one answer to that, and I gave it.

Jacky, when he learned of our future, had one other thing to add. "I guess I can't call you 'Father' any more. I guess I'll have to call you 'Pa'."

ACKNOWLEDGMENTS

My thanks to Emory Cantey for providing me details on glass plate photography and the difficulties of developing in the field.

Always, I thank my husband Glenn for his knowledge of the West, his editorial suggestions, and for putting up with me during the writing.

ABOUT THE AUTHOR

Born and raised near Pittsburgh, Pennsylvania, **Jane Candia Coleman** majored in creative writing at the University of Pittsburgh but stopped writing after graduation in 1960 because she knew she "hadn't lived enough, thought enough, to write anything of interest." Her life changed dramatically when she abandoned the East for the West in 1986, and her creativity came truly into its own. *The Voices of Doves* (1988) was written soon after she moved to Tucson. It was followed by a book of poetry, *No Roof But Sky* (1990), and by a truly remarkable short story collection that amply repays reading and re-reading, *Stories From Mesa Country* (1991). Her short story, "Lou" in *Louis L'Amour Western Magazine* (3/94), won the Spur Award from the Western Writers of America as did her later short story, "Are You Coming Back, Phin Montana?" in *Louis L'Amour Magazine* (1/96). She has also won three Western Heritage Awards from the National Cowboy Hall of Fame. *Doc Holliday's Woman* (1995) was her first novel and one of vivid and extraordinary power. The highly acclaimed *Moving On: Stories of the West* was her first **Five Star Western,** and it contains her two Spur award-winning stories. It was followed in 1998 with the novel, *I, Pearl Hart,* and then her novel, *The O'Keefe Empire* (Five Star Westerns, 1999). Other story collections include *Borderlands* (Five Star Westerns, 2000) and *Country Music* (Five Star Westerns, 2002). It can be said that a story by Jane Candia Coleman embodies the essence of what is finest in the Western story, intimations of hope, vulnerability, and courage, while she plummets to the depths of her characters, conjuring moods and imagery with the consummate artistry of an accomplished poet.

The employees of Thorndike Press hope you have enjoyed this Large Print book. All our Thorndike, Wheeler, and Kennebec Large Print titles are designed for easy reading, and all our books are made to last. Other Thorndike Press Large Print books are available at your library, through selected bookstores, or directly from us.

For information about titles, please call:
  (800) 223-1244

or visit our Web site at:
  http://gale.cengage.com/thorndike

To share your comments, please write:
  Publisher
  Thorndike Press
  10 Water St., Suite 310
  Waterville, ME 04901